A GUIDE TO THE OTHER SIDE

A Beyond Baylor Novel

A GUIDE TO THE OTHER SIDE

ROBERT IMFELD

Aladdin

New York   London   Toronto   Sydney   New Delhi

ALADDIN
An imprint of Simon & Schuster Children's Publishing Division
1230 Avenue of the Americas, New York, New York 10020
First Aladdin hardcover edition October 2016
Text copyright © 2016 by Robert Imfeld
Jacket illustration copyright © 2016 by Hugh D'Andrade
All rights reserved, including the right of reproduction
in whole or in part in any form.
ALADDIN is a trademark of Simon & Schuster, Inc., and related logo
is a registered trademark of Simon & Schuster, Inc.
For information about special discounts for bulk purchases, please contact
Simon & Schuster Special Sales at 1-866-506-1949 or business@simonandschuster.com.
The Simon & Schuster Speakers Bureau can bring authors to your live event.
For more information or to book an event, contact the Simon & Schuster Speakers Bureau
at 1-866-248-3049 or visit our website at www.simonspeakers.com.
Jacket designed by Karin Paprocki
Interior designed by Mike Rosamilia
The text of this book was set in Centaur MT Std.
Manufactured in the United States of America 0916 FFG
2 4 6 8 10 9 7 5 3 1
Library of Congress Cataloging-in-Publication Data
Names: Imfeld, Robert, author.
Title: A guide to the other side / Robert Imfeld.
Description: First Aladdin hardcover edition. | New York : Aladdin, 2016. |
Series: A Beyond Baylor novel | Summary: Thirteen-year-old Baylor Bosco does not like ghosts,
but as a medium he sees them—including his twin sister, Kristina—everywhere, but Kristina
disappears after a strange ghost shows up and Baylor must try to find her on his own.
Identifiers: LCCN 2015050806 (print) | LCCN 2016024871 (eBook) | ISBN 9781481466363 (hc) |
ISBN 9781481466370 (pbk) | ISBN 9781481466387 (eBook) |
Subjects: | CYAC: Mediums—Fiction. | Ghosts—Fiction. | Brothers and sisters—Fiction. | Twins—
Fiction. | Mystery and detective stories. | BISAC: JUVENILE FICTION / Mysteries &
Detective Stories. | JUVENILE FICTION / Family / Siblings. | JUVENILE FICTION /
Horror & Ghost Stories. Classification: LCC PZ7.1.I4 Gui 2016 (print) | LCC PZ7.1.I4 (eBook) |
DDC [Fic]—dc23 | LC record available at https://lccn.loc.gov/2015050806

To Mom and Dad—
the first readers, the biggest fans,
and the best parents

A
GUIDE TO THE
OTHER SIDE

1

A good routine is KEY.

MY DAY CAN'T BEGIN WITHOUT MY ROUTINE.

1. Wake up and light a candle. (I prefer a simple white candle, though I've been known to shake it up during the holidays and use a pine scent.) I breathe deeply and encircle myself with positive energy.

This first step is crucial to having a good day.

2. Check my dream journal to see if I scrawled any messages in the middle of the night. (There are a couple of lines on the page sometimes, but I'm pretty good at remembering my dreams, not to brag or anything.)

3. Check in with my twin, Kristina, and ask her how her night was.

4. Ask for only good vibes to emanate from the Beyond before I blow out my candle and start my day.

A chilly Thursday morning just two days before Halloween, the worst holiday ever created, I lit seven candles and placed them around me, creating a fiery barrier. I'd been doing the same thing at night, too, for the past week. Halloween may be fun for everyone else, but for someone who can communicate with ghosts, I can assure you it's not fun at all. Halloween is the one time of year where it can be tricky to control the malevolent spirits. So many of them try to break through, even if I ensure through my protections they can't communicate with me directly. It's all because of the morons who wear those grotesque, bloody masks and costumes without realizing the very real effect it has on my life.

Those costumes summon negative energy, and I can literally feel the forces floating around, circling me like sharks around a bloody seal. Kristina hates Halloween more than I do. I can forbid those spirits from entering my vision, but she can't, so while I'm walking down the street, choosing to be oblivious, she's turning left and right, looking at one horror after the next. I don't envy her.

It was on our walk to school that she mentioned how it was getting pretty bad already.

"Everyone must have tried on their costumes last night," she said. "You would not believe how many murderers and politicians we're passing."

"Are they saying anything to you?" I asked. My shoes crunched up the yellow leaves that covered the sidewalk.

"No, they're mostly grunting a lot. They know not to mess with us."

"I still don't get how they know that. Who would come rocketing over to this side to punish them?"

"I'm not entirely sure, but I know it would be bad," she said. "I think it's better not to know."

She was wrong. I wanted to know so bad. She always said stuff like that to me: "We're not permitted to know that yet," "We haven't learned enough to earn that knowledge." It was so frustrating that I couldn't grab her and shake more information out of her like I could with my little brother, Jack.

"Can you hear that?" she asked.

"Yeah." Some man was screaming about a lost dog, but I'd been awake for only twenty minutes and didn't want to deal with ghosts yet. "Does he expect me to knock on his wife's door and deliver a message for him? He knows that's not how this works."

"Give him a second," Kristina said lightly.

Three seconds later a door opened two houses ahead, and a woman walked out wearing a green bathrobe and pink slippers. Her arms were clenched across her chest, and she was looking around, confused.

"Why did I come out here again?" she mumbled.

Kristina raised an eyebrow at me, and I rolled my eyes and muttered, "It's too early for this," before I slouched my way up to the woman and said, "Excuse me, ma'am?" She turned my way and looked at me like I'd just personally caused her dog to run away.

"Yes, young man?"

"My name is Baylor Bosco, and I can communicate with people who have crossed over." I must have repeated that exact sentence more than two thousand times by now. "Your husband wanted me to let you know that your dog is with him on the other side now, and, well, it's time to move on, Trish. The animal shelter has a small brown terrier he thinks you might like."

I braced myself for her reaction. I might have done this more than two thousand times by now, but I was never sure how people would react. I got off easy this time, though. The woman's mouth dropped open, and her eyes filled with tears.

"How did you know that?" she asked. They always

ask that too, even though I've just told them I can communicate with dead people.

"I was born with a gift," I said, shrugging. "Oh, he also wants me to tell you that you need to change the curtains because they're hideous."

"That is just like him to say." She laughed so heartily that I found myself wishing everyone would react as well to weird messages like that. "Is he doing okay?"

I nodded. "Just fine."

Then I kept on walking. Normally, I would engage with the alive person more, but her husband was still shouting nonsense in our ears and I needed him to stop. It was 7:30 a.m., and no one, dead or alive, should have permission to scream that early. After I broke the connection, the shouting stopped, as it always did after I shared a healing message. It was Kristina's job to seal the ghosts on the other side and make sure they no longer disturbed us.

It might seem harsh, but some of them just don't get it. I'm here to relay the message, and it's not up to me whether the person on the receiving end listens or not. When I first started delivering messages, before Kristina helped me tune out most spirits, I'd have these horribly persistent ones poking me over and over to deliver the same message I'd just passed along.

"They didn't believe you, you need to go back over and try again," they'd say.

Later Kristina established a rule with the ghosts: If you're going to use Baylor to deliver a message, you've got only one shot to deliver it. They could come back with a different message, and that'd be fine, just as long as it wasn't the same one.

"He was loud," I grunted. I hadn't slept well last night because I kept getting ruffled by some ghost children who passed through my room.

"*You* think it's loud? Try being on this side of the fence. The man was practically screaming in my ear."

"Your nonexistent ghost ears?"

"Shut up, they hear better than yours do."

Oh, there's one important detail to know about Kristina—she's dead.

2

Imaginary friends and dead twin sisters aren't the same thing.

MOST PEOPLE DON'T BELIEVE ME WHEN I TELL them my sister's ghost accompanies me through life, but it's true. Well, I take that back. Most people don't believe me *at first*. The only reason I can see my sister in the first place is because I can talk to all dead people, so usually there's a talkative aunt or a doting grandma around who can help me deliver a persuasive message to the doubters. My sister, though, was never born. We were in the womb together, hanging out and growing cells, when one day her body fell apart.

I was born just fine, and early on I had no idea I didn't have a real, live sister. She was always beside me, talking to me and playing with me and even fighting with me. My parents thought I just had an extremely active imagination, complete with an extremely realistic imaginary friend.

When I was five years old, I mentioned something to my mom.

"Mommy," I said, "how come you never talk to Kristina?"

"Kristina's your imaginary friend, honey," my mom said for the hundredth time. "I can't see or speak to her."

"But she was in your belly with me," I said. "She told me she was. She said you cried for days after you lost her, but you didn't lose her, because she's right there."

I pointed to my smiling twin sitting in her chair at the kitchen table, rays of sun shooting through the wide window but not quite bouncing off her curly golden hair. I didn't realize the look on my mom's face was one of horror. It simply didn't register with me that she would be stunned to find out her son's imaginary friend was no friend at all, but rather her miscarried daughter.

"Baylor," she said slowly, "how do you know you

had a twin? Did you overhear Daddy or Grandma talking about it?"

"No, Mommy!" I said, so frustrated she wasn't getting it. "She *told* me."

"Baylor, tell her that the envelope she's missing fell between the desk and the filing cabinet," Kristina said, giggling.

"And," I said, "she told me to tell you that the missing envelope fell between the desk and the filing cabinet."

My mom's face transformed from horror to confusion to panic. She left me at the table and sprinted to the home office, then returned a moment later holding an insurance document she'd apparently misplaced weeks earlier.

I saw her hands shaking violently, but I didn't know what that meant. Now that I'm older—thirteen, in fact—I see those shaky hands a lot, and I try to be as empathetic as possible when relaying messages to people from their loved ones. People can't help but feel scared when confronted with this sort of supernatural activity.

After my mom found the letter, she sobbed for an hour, then finally pulled herself together and asked my dad to come home from work. She wouldn't say why, but since my mom was pregnant with my brother, he thought something bad had happened. When he burst through the door, he found my mom a blubbering mess at the table, and he found me sitting on the kitchen floor, pushing my fire truck along the tiles while Kristina made loud siren noises next to me.

They talked for a bit, and then my dad walked over to me in the funniest way, like I was a snake that had gotten loose in the house and he was trying to catch me. He crouched down slowly in front of me and took a big gulp.

"Hey, buddy. Mommy told me about your imaginary friend," he said. I'll never forget how his knees wavered as he talked to me, like he couldn't find his balance.

"Kristina's not my friend, she's my sister, Daddy," I said, barely looking over. I didn't get why they were making such a big deal out of it. I didn't get why they didn't just love her like they loved me. I had never noticed until a few days before that they never tucked her in, or set a plate for her at dinner, or hung her drawings up, or even had a bed for her. I thought that was pretty mean. "She's sitting right there."

I pointed to the space in front of the fridge, and of course my dad saw nothing. But to me, she was as fully formed and normal as any of my new kindergarten friends were. There was one difference, though, which I had spotted even back then as a little boy: The only way to know for sure if a person is a ghost is to watch his or her eyes.

Ghosts don't blink. They just stare at you like they're trying to break the record for the world's creepiest staring contest. You'd think there'd be more obvious ways to tell if people are dead or alive, but there's really not. They don't breathe, of course, but it's not like it's easy to tell if people are breathing when they're just standing there. And they're not transparent, either, as much as the movies like to think they are. They're as normal-looking as the next person . . . well, most of them, anyway.

My dad looked at the empty space and back at me and then back at the empty space.

"Baylor, buddy, you're telling me you see a little girl sitting right there right now?" he said, trying his best to laugh.

"He doesn't think I'm here," Kristina said sadly. At the time she also didn't totally grasp the fact that she wasn't alive.

"I know," I said, frowning at her. "I don't know why."

"Tell him Mommy's baby is another boy, so he doesn't have to worry about having a girl yet."

I told him what she'd said, and his mouth dropped open and his face kind of fell forward.

"Another boy?" my mom squeaked from the table. "Oh! Good!"

It would take another month for the doctor to be able to confirm that the baby was, in fact, a boy, and when they came home from the doctor's office that day, they were walking on eggshells around me.

Looking back, I now realize how scared they were.

At school Kristina tends to keep to herself. She follows me around, but she knows I can't sit there and talk to her. I don't try to hide my gift, and although most of the kids at school know what I can do, they don't really know about Kristina. It would just be too odd to have a full-on conversation with someone that nobody else can see or hear.

School that day was so slow. For a few periods I thought maybe some evil spirits were playing a trick on me and slowing the clock down. I even excused myself during one class, hid in a bathroom stall, and lit my emergency lighter while casting away all negative energy.

Kristina giggled from outside the stall.

"It's not funny, Kristina," I said, the flame still lit as I envisioned myself covered in light.

"Actually, it is," she said back. "Nobody's doing anything to you. It's just a boring day."

By lunchtime I was ready to fall asleep, and I still couldn't shake the feeling that a spirit was at fault. At the lunch table I put my head down on my arms and closed my eyes.

"You okay, man?" my friend Aiden asked. We'd been pals since fifth grade, when I joined the band in elementary school. I was a band geek by choice, and Aiden was a band geek by default. He played the flute, was pudgy, and had terrible acne, and I was almost positive his mom cut his hair, though I'd never asked. But he was my best and most loyal blinking friend, and he'd stuck by me even after finding out my other best friend was my dead twin sister.

"I've been feeling terrible all day," I said.

"Is it because Halloween's soon?" he asked, opening his red lunch box and unpacking a pepperoni sandwich. "I know all the poltergeists come out to play this time of year."

I shot him a look. "I'm actually sort of worried that might be the case."

"Oh, sorry, man," he said. He took a bite of his sandwich, and a glob of mustard oozed down his chin. "Kristina hasn't done anything to help you?"

"How can I help you when I'm too busy watching

this mess try to eat?" Kristina said from next to me on the bench. I chuckled, causing Aiden to furrow his eyebrows.

"What's so funny?"

"Nothing, nothing," I said. "She said it isn't a spirit, so maybe I'm just being paranoid."

We changed the subject when two other band members came to sit with us. Plus, I wanted to try to forget about my weird spirit problems, if only for a few minutes.

The rest of the day passed in a blur, and when the final bell rang, I texted Aiden and told him I was skipping band practice because I needed to get home and rest. I almost always walked to and from school—it's barely over a mile away from my house—but today I called my mom and asked her to pick me up.

"You're being such a baby, Baylor," Kristina said. "I know you're not sick."

"Then why do I feel so bad?" I leaned back against the brick wall of the admin building and curled myself into a ball.

"I'm not sure."

"Well, if you can't make it stop, then you're not allowed to have an opinion." Maybe I was imagining it, but even the sky seemed darker—a dull, lifeless gray.

My mom arrived a few minutes later, and I opened the front door of her black SUV to climb in.

"What's wrong, honey?" she said. "Is it a fever?" She held the back of her hand to my forehead and frowned, making almost the same face as Kristina, though I didn't tell her that. It was still weird that she didn't know what her own daughter looked like, despite talking to her every day.

"I don't think it's a fever," I said. "I'm not sure what it is. I just feel terrible."

"Let's get you home," she said. "Did you say hi to Ella yet?"

When I was eleven, my parents welcomed a wonderful little accident named Ella into the world. To me and Kristina, though, she was no accident at all, as I reminded them when they told me Mom was pregnant.

"Remember what I told Dad when I talked to you both about Kristina?" I said. "'He doesn't have to worry about having a girl *yet*.' I told you both about her six years ago!"

The look of shock on my dad's face grew exponentially worse after realizing it was going to be a girl. He had raised two boys so far. What the heck was he going to do with a little girl?

But it wasn't something he had to worry about,

because Ella soon had him wrapped around her little finger. And I have to admit, I was right there with him. She was the cutest little thing I'd ever seen.

Plus, there was the whole fact that she could see spirits. Actually, most babies can—Jack was one of the twitchiest babies ever because of it—but Ella's ability seemed to be amplified thanks to me and Kristina working so well as a team. She couldn't communicate with them, and her ability would fade away in a couple years, but for now she could interact with Kristina and see the same spirits I could.

"Hi, baby Ella," I said, looking at her through the rearview mirror. I was too exhausted to turn my body around. "Seen any scary spirits today?"

She smiled widely at me for a second before turning her attention back to the baby doll she was holding. She had the most squeezable cheeks of any one-and-a-half-year-old I'd ever met, and they were soon to be overtaken by her ultracurly hair. Now that she was out of her late-night crying phase of life, I loved Ella a ton.

"Did . . . did Kristina say anything about your being sick?" my mom asked. She always spoke in a hushed tone when it came to Kristina, who could hear just fine at any volume.

"Nope, doesn't know a thing," I said. "Really helpful."

Kristina was probably happy Mom had asked after her, but the thought of turning to look at her made me queasy.

When we got back home, I essentially crawled upstairs and found Kristina already in my room with her arms crossed.

"You're starting to worry me," she said. "It must be all the Halloween energy. What else could it be?"

"It's never affected me like this before, though," I said.

"Maybe things are changing." She almost sounded excited. "Maybe I need to have a talk with one of my spirit guides tonight while you sleep."

"Please do. I'll take all the help I can get."

Without another word I passed out.

I woke with a start hours later, but I couldn't see the clock. It was dark outside, but the light was still on from earlier.

"Kristina?" I called out.

No response. I thought that was weird but remembered she was going to talk to her guides. Feeling better about her absence, I reached over to turn the lamp off.

When the room went dark, a horrible chill passed through every pore of my body. I sat up in bed, shivering, and in the corner of my room, right in front of the window, stood a man with a white sheet draped over his head.

He seemed very tall, but that could have been because I was in bed. He was perfectly still, almost like a statue, and the edge of the sheet was precisely ruffled like a coiled snake near the floor. Most people would have screamed, but I've experienced some weird things in my day.

But then I noticed the eyes. They were two small holes in the sheet, just big enough for the pupils, and even through the dark all I saw was shiny black pools of menace staring right at me. I forgot how to use my lungs, and as I gasped for air, it felt like the world was closing in on me. The second I saw those eyes, I knew something was wrong.

An evil spirit had breached my barrier.

TIP

3

Do not panic.

"BE GONE, SPIRIT!" I SHOUTED, BUT IT DIDN'T move. The eyes gleamed like black sulfur, but it still made no motion. The sheet didn't sway an inch.

I reached out for my lamp and clicked it on, and as the light filled the room, the demon vanished. A final chill overtook my body, and I exhaled heavily. I looked down and saw my hands shaking.

"Baylor!" Kristina shouted as she materialized from nowhere. "What happened? I couldn't access your room. One second I was here, and the next I was trapped outside."

I turned to her, and I'm sure my face was as white as the sheet that had covered that man.

"Baylor, it's okay," she said as she sat on my bed. "It's over. Whatever happened, it's over. Tell me what you saw."

I looked at my hands, unable to quell the shaking.

"It was some sort of terrible spirit, Kristina," I finally said. "I turned the light off, and a person wearing a white sheet was standing in the corner. His eyes, Kristina . . . it was like the devil was looking at me."

"Then what happened?"

"I told him to leave, and when he wouldn't go, I turned the light back on and he disappeared, and then you came back, and now we're talking, and my hands won't stop shaking."

"Demon dung!" she said, her voice hushed. "I need to speak with my guides right away."

"No! Don't go. What if he comes back?"

"Light some candles," she said. "Place them all around the house and ask for more good spirits to stand guard."

I nodded. "Okay, I'll go get some from downstairs."

"That will keep whatever it was at bay for now." She paused for a moment, looking at my shaking hands. "Whatever it was, Baylor, it was really bad.

I'm surrounded by positive energy, just as you are, and I couldn't even share the same space as it. I've never encountered anything like it before."

"Forget the candles," I said, springing out of bed. "I'm lighting the fireplace, and the grill, and I'm going to find a freaking torch to carry around."

After I had secured the premises with the candles—placing a few extras in Ella's room—I dug through the china cabinet in the dining room. I found what I was looking for tucked away behind the plastic plates and rolled-up tablecloths: a four-wick candle. My mom kept a few candles like this for special occasions, and I was pretty sure tonight qualified as more special than her boring book club.

With all four wicks lit, I went back up to my room feeling like I was holding a nuclear bomb. *Try and get me now, Sheet Man!* Whatever that thing was, it wouldn't be back. Not tonight, anyway.

Even so, I couldn't shake the image of those black eyes. It was bad enough seeing an exaggerated version of the classic ghost—*oh, a sheet over your head, super original*—but to see it unmoving and unblinking and unspeaking, with those deadened, haunting eyes? I felt threatened. Someone or something was trying to intimidate me, in my own home no less, and I didn't like it.

* * *

"They have no idea how it happened," Kristina said the next morning, fresh from a powwow with her spirit guides. "The fact that I couldn't be around it made them all incredibly nervous. They're setting up extra protection around the house."

"Well, that's good," I said. "Except now I'm more freaked out than I was last night. Shouldn't your spirit guides know everything? Isn't that what they're there for?"

"They know everything about *us*," she said. "Not random evil spirits who make you wet your bed, Baylor."

"I didn't wet my bed, Kristina."

"I'm not convinced."

"You're dead. You can go back and relive that moment."

"But it's so much more fun this way."

I shook my head. "This isn't funny, you know. That thing could have sucked up my soul or unleashed demon spiders on me or something." I shuddered at the thought of demon spiders descending from the ceiling and crawling all over me.

"Listen, Baylor, I know you're nervous, but it was a onetime thing. You'll have so much energy surrounding you today, it'll be like you're wearing a suit of armor."

"Well, that sounds good, I guess."

"Just try not to pee in it if you get a little nervous."

I didn't learn a single thing at school that day. I just kept tossing around the possible intentions of the Sheet Man's visit.

Was he actually threatening me? Sure, his eyes were freaky, but other than that, was he really that scary? Physically, no. But the fact that his presence had obstructed Kristina from sharing the room was alarming at best, and a harbinger of my impending death at worst.

Maybe he was just keeping watch over me in a way Kristina couldn't? I had been building up my positive energy so much for Halloween that it was difficult for me to accept that any sort of bad spirit could have broken through. Who's to say that he wasn't merely a sentinel with a sheet?

It was also possible he was trying to send a message. What if he needed help? What if some corrupt company was selling a brand of sheets that would somehow strangle people in their sleep? What if a bunch of children overseas were locked in a factory and being forced to fabricate the sheets? What if it wasn't a sheet at all and he was just a fashionable ghost? Unlikely, but since I could talk to dead people, I didn't like to rule out unlikely things.

By the end of the day I had resolved to do a little investigating. Since I was fairly confident it had been a sheet and not some sort of ghostly burka, I decided to go straight to the source and take the bus to Bed Bath & Beyond. It was practically sheet heaven. I figured maybe I could find a similar white sheet, which might lead to a clue.

Riding a bus, or a plane or a train or, well, any kind of transportation where I'm trapped with strangers, can be a very unpredictable experience for me. Sometimes the passengers around me will be boring and, in turn, have boring loved ones who won't bother me.

Other times it's pure chaos.

The only thing I can compare it to is when you're walking along a street and a jackhammer is pounding into the pavement. That deafening, grating noise is all you can hear, and you can try to ignore it and talk over it, but it's just too loud.

Ghosts, especially the pesky ones, are my personal jackhammers pounding relentlessly into my brain. They will get in my face and yell at me until I deliver a message. Even when I try to tune them out, they'll scream from the other side, and eventually Kristina will get so annoyed with them that she'll force me to deliver the message just so she can break the connection and seal off the ghost.

It's really bad when there's more than one of these annoying ghosts, who always have the most inane messages. Stupid things like "She needs to remember to change the air conditioner filters more often" or "He needs to know that I'm okay with him throwing out all my socks." I could understand the urgency if the ghosts died tragically and they wished to tell a loved one that they were now at peace, or maybe they knew of a dark secret the person was keeping and they wished to give that person comfort. In those kinds of situations I'm almost always happy to help.

But when I have a small Venezuelan woman yammering in my ear that her granddaughter is using the incorrect arepa recipe and, thus, embarrassing her family's legacy, I'm not so pleased to relay the message.

Kristina, who's learned a lot alongside me over the years, once told me my purpose was to deliver healing messages, and if I didn't think a message was healing, I didn't need to deliver it. That's also why I'm able to tune out certain spirits.

But sometimes the ghosts are so strong and persistent that it's easier to give in.

"My name is Baylor Bosco, and I can communicate with people who have crossed over," I finally blurted out to the haggard-looking woman in the seat behind me. "I'm so sorry to have to tell you this, but your grandma will not stop pestering me. She says you're using the wrong kind of cornmeal in your arepas and that you're tarnishing her reputation every time you serve them to people and tell them that you used her recipe."

"Jor makin' me look bad, *chiquita*," the grandma lamented.

The woman blinked at me.

"Did you understand me?" I said slowly.

"Yes, I understood you," she said, shaking her head. "Shut up and turn around."

Ugh. A doubter.

"I'm not kidding, Ana."

Her eyebrows shot up.

"How'd you know my name?"

"Your grandma told me. She's standing right there." I pointed to the space just over her shoulder, where her grandma hovered, clucking her tongue as she examined her hair.

Her eyes followed my finger, but she saw nothing, of course. She looked around the bus, this time with a slight grin on her face. "Did Armando put you up to this?" She chuckled. "I'm gonna be on YouTube, aren't I?" She waved to the nonexistent hidden cameras while sticking out her tongue.

"No," I said, shaking my head. "It's just me, you, and your annoyed *abuela*."

"Do me a favah," the old woman said. "Tell Ana her hair looked bettah when it was dyed blue, not this nasty pink like it is now."

I repeated the message, and Ana's face collapsed into a frown.

"Oh." She looked out the window. "That sounds just like something she'd say. I got it done yesterday."

"She needs to go get her money back!"

I looked at the old woman. "I'm not saying that."

"What'd she say?" Ana asked, her head whipping back in my direction.

I sighed. "She said you should go get your money back."

"I thought people were supposed to get nicer after they died."

"Most of them do," I said.

Still frowning, her voice a bit terse, she asked, "What's the right cornmeal, then?"

"She says it's Masarepa flour, not masa harina, because that has lime in it and makes the arepas taste *malas*."

I can't speak Spanish, but that's a funny thing about communicating with ghosts. Even though I speak with them in English, whenever I relay a message to their loved ones, a part of their personality and soul can also come through.

I turned to Kristina and nodded. My work here was done, and a second later the woman had disappeared.

"Did she say anything else?" Ana asked. "Did she mention my fiancé? Does she like Armando?"

My lips pressed together awkwardly. "I'm not sure. She just left."

"Typical," she muttered, rolling her eyes. "Do me a favor: Next time keep my grandma's messages to yourself."

Inside Bed Bath & Beyond, I wandered around looking for the bedding department, bewildered by all the products I never knew existed. There were so many different kinds of pots and pans and baking sheets and knives and kitchen utensils. There was an entire wall of pillows, soaring up to the ceiling some twenty feet high. How were people supposed to see the pillows at the very top? Not everyone had a ghost sister who could drift up and give her opinion.

Once my shock wore away and I found the right section of the store, I realized it would be no easy task to find the correct white sheet, mostly because there were about two billion styles to choose from.

"Can you sense anything?" I asked Kristina. I was perusing the rows, one by one, touching every single package in the hope that some sort of message would be attached to one of them. Sometimes I can see a memory associated with an object. The problem is that there doesn't seem to be any real rhyme or reason to these visions, so I'll find myself randomly touching something and gasping in shock when a memory takes over. I've learned to avoid antique shops.

"Nothing," she said. "We're on a wild-goose chase here, Baylor. That sheet could have been purchased from anywhere, and that's if the sheet matters at all, which I can almost guarantee you it doesn't."

"There has to be something else that we're not getting, Kristina," I said. "It doesn't make any sense that he'd stand in the corner and not say a single word."

"He was probably trying to scare you," she said. "It's Halloween. Spirits like to have fun too. Especially the evil ones."

I shook my head. "I have a weird feeling about this. I don't know what the feeling is or why I think it's weird, I just know I have it."

A woman with auburn hair, who'd been examining a white comforter with red flowers on it, was glancing at me, her eyes filled with concern. When I was younger, I used to blush whenever people caught me speaking to Kristina, since I knew they thought I was crazy and speaking out loud to myself. But time heals everything, and I nodded as I passed her.

"Happy Halloween," I said. "Watch out for the evil spirits."

When I got back home, my mom asked where I'd been.

"Just doing some shopping," I said.

"For what? Are you actually going to dress up this year?" Her face had lit up from behind the counter, where she was dicing an onion. She was always so disappointed that I refused to participate in Halloween. All the other moms got cute pictures every year of their children dressed as ninjas and Bugs Bunny and clowns, and all she got was a kid who preferred to spend Halloween night wandering around a cemetery with his dead sister.

"Sorry to disappoint you," I said, "but no."

"Come on, Baylor!" she pleaded. "You're thirteen. This will probably be the last year you can get away with trick-or-treating. No one wants to give candy away to a guy who has to shave."

I sighed. "I don't care about Halloween, Mom, you know that."

"I know, I know," she said. She threw the onions into

the frying pan, and they hissed and smoked. "I just don't want you to regret anything when you're older."

A part of me wondered if she was right. I hadn't dressed up for Halloween since I was at least eight, and I couldn't remember ever having gone trick-or-treating, mostly because I couldn't imagine being on the street and not knowing who was alive and who was a ghost . . . or worse.

"Maybe I'll text Aiden and ask what he's doing tomorrow," I said. "If only so you can have one picture of me, Jack, and Ella dressed up for Halloween."

My mom dropped the spoon she was using, and her eyes welled up.

"Would you really do that for me?"

Oh no. I hadn't really been serious, but now that the thought of a single photograph had made her cry, how could I backtrack?

"Uh, yeah, of course," I said.

Sitting on the couch in the family room, I texted Aiden.

BAYLOR: Got any plans for tomorrow?

AIDEN: Me, bobby and j are
gonna trick or treat around my
neighborhood

BAYLOR: Care if I come?

AIDEN: You serious? I didn't tell you about it only cuz you reject me every year

BAYLOR: I changed my mind this year

AIDEN: YES. Meet at my house at 7

All I had to do was find a costume.

Beware: Halloween is more tricks than treats.

I KNEW IF I COULDN'T AVOID THE MASSES on Halloween night, I'd need to pick a costume that increased my protection by its very nature. No bloody masks or devil horns for me. I racked my brain for ideas and even asked Kristina what she thought.

"An angel, of course," she said.

"I can't go as an angel! I'll look ridiculous, and not in a good way!"

"No spirits would bother you, though."

"I'm not dressing as an angel. Any other ideas?"

I rejected going as a priest, a nun, a Greek god

(too cold for togas), a (friendly) clown, and a doctor before I finally settled on something that was both funny and positive: a baby.

The next day I went to Wal-Mart and found giant pink footed pajamas, which were perfect for the cold night ahead, as well as adult diapers to put over them.

But just walking through Wal-Mart gave me some second thoughts about trick-or-treating. Though I had lit all my candles that morning, it was clear the negative Halloween energy was starting to infringe on my positive energy, because I could see some dark spirits floating around me. They didn't disturb me, since they knew they couldn't touch me, but they stuck close to the people they'd attached themselves to. I asked Kristina to show me the auras of those people, one of her handy tricks.

"Brace yourself," she said grimly.

An aura is the outward reflection of a living person's soul, and these people were in dire straits. Their bodies glowed nearly black—but in the radioactive, toxic-waste sense of the word "glow." Their souls were tarnished from those dark spirits, and it made me shudder to think of some of the even more evil spirits lurking around me that hadn't yet attached themselves to people.

Spirits can be really different from ghosts. Ghosts

are the souls of dead people wandering about, while a spirit can be any sort of nonliving supernatural entity. It's like that miserable square-and-rectangle math rule: All ghosts are spirits, but not all spirits are ghosts. You'll never hear me say an evil ghost is lurking around. As Kristina used to say, "Ghosts are good, but spirits need speculation!"

A ghost would never leech on to a living person's aura, but an evil spirit would. And the longer it leeched, the more powerful it became. One woman in particular had such a dark aura that I couldn't even see her face properly. She was shrouded in darkness, and it was obvious why. An Ashen, the name for a newly formed demon, was sucking away her energy. Just based on the darkness of her aura, I'd bet a hundred bucks this Ashen had used her to transform from a regular old evil spirit to a demon, the evil version of a caterpillar becoming a butterfly. A disgusting, wretched butterfly.

I felt the need to help her, so I found the candle aisle, grabbed a few small white ones, and tracked her down near the checkout line. When the Ashen noticed me, its face went rigid. The demon's lower half was as billowy and misshapen as smoke, giving way to a solid top half that was shrouded in loose black material. Its face was, in so many words, pointy and deformed. The chin was a sharp triangle, so sharp that poking it with my finger would draw blood. Its cheeks were scaly and sunken, and the forehead was big enough that you could sell advertising space on it for a nice profit.

And those awful eyes—unblinking furnaces of burning green. They'd turn red one day.

"Ma'am," I whispered, looking at the demon, trying in vain to block it out. She turned to me, looking confused, since my eyes weren't focused on her.

"You talking to me, kid?"

"You need to buy these candles, light the wicks, and imagine the light of the flames surrounding your body." The demon roared with anger upon hearing my words, and I backed up a few feet.

"Baylor, it can't hurt you," Kristina reminded me. She was standing between me and the Ashen, her arms crossed and her eyes also scanning the creature. I wondered for a second if it could hurt her.

The woman narrowed her eyes at me. "What are you talking about, kid? I'm gonna call security on you if you don't get away from me."

I was still staring at the demon, which almost appeared to smirk, but that's nonsense, since demons don't smirk. As quickly as I could move, I pulled out my lighter, lit a candle, and sent the light her way.

Like a rope cut by a white-hot sword, the demon detached with a terrible hiss as the light enveloped the woman.

Now that the demon was no longer attached to a person, I could easily block it from my view with Kristina's help.

"Much better," I said, sighing with relief. I raised my eyebrows at Kristina and did a little jig with my feet. Nothing like banishing a demon to really get your day going.

"What did you just do to me?" the woman asked. She wasn't mad, though. In fact, whereas she had been hunched over just a moment ago, she now stood nearly a foot higher. "I haven't felt this great in years!"

"That does not surprise me." I blew out the candle and handed the armful over. "Buy the candles. Do what I told you. You'll need it." Demons always find a way back into people's lives. It's up to them whether they choose to fight the demons or let them wreak havoc.

She took the candles, thanked me, and walked off. Kristina nodded her approval.

"Nice one," she said. "You're making excellent progress."

"What does that mean?" I asked.

"Oh, nothing," she said casually.

* * *

Back at home I finished the costume with one of Ella's bibs and an old rattle.

When I checked myself in the mirror, I smiled. It was perfect.

"You have never looked this dumb," Kristina said crossly, her hands on her hips. "I know you're supposed to be a baby, but you're not a cute baby. You're an overgrown monster of a baby, and I think it's only going to attract negative energy."

"I think you're jealous," I said, turning to admire the way my butt looked in that diaper. "This costume can't bring me anything but good vibes."

She shook her head. "At least Mom'll be happy."

And she was right. When my mom saw the costume, she actually started jumping.

"Stay right there!" she yelled. "I need to get my nice camera." She ran away for a moment, returning with her massive DSLR camera, and she proceeded to take a hundred pictures of me standing there, dressed as a giant pink baby.

"You look so good! I need to get Jack and Ella ready so they can jump in too."

A couple of hours later my mom was getting the pictures she'd dreamed about for years in front of our sparsely decorated house.

We live in a nice neighborhood in Keene, a boring city in New Hampshire. All the houses on our street are old and give off that classic New England feel, with slatted wood, pillars, and stoops galore. Around Halloween most of our neighbors go crazy with their decorations. They put cobwebs and little white, cartoony ghosts in their trees. They hang big, hairy spiders around their doorways and plant bloody zombie hands in the soil. Witches on brooms seem to be very popular, and there's always a few that feature the witch smashed headfirst into the side of the house—exactly what witches deserve, if you ask me.

Not our house. Except for a small orange sign that says HAPPY HALLOWEEN! and the occasional jack-o'-lantern (carved only with happy faces), you'll never know it's the season of goblins and ghouls at the Bosco residence. I forbade my parents from hanging up any decorations long ago, much to my mom's displeasure. She used to love Halloween, but now that she had a child who could see those ghouls people usually only joked about, she'd had to stifle her affection for the holiday.

"Jack, smile for this next picture!" Mom said as we shivered in front of the house. Keene isn't exactly known for its warmth and sun in the winter, but with highs in the thirties, it was unseasonably cold even for our frigid little town.

"I can't feel my face!" he said. "Maybe I should put on last year's costume. That one had a mask." He was dressed up as a soldier from one of his favorite movies. Last year he'd been a dinosaur.

Ella was a princess, and a very cute one at that, with a pink tiara, a gold dress, and little pink shoes. Kristina was staring off into the distance near an almost bare tree, a few scattered leaves still clinging to the branches.

"You look good!" my mom said. "You'll just have to run from house to house to stay warm!"

"Dad's gonna love that," I said, tickling baby Ella to make her laugh. My dad goes around with Jack every year while my mom stays home and passes out candy.

I usually go to the cemetery. It's the most peaceful place to be on Halloween night, and the one place where spirits almost never hang around. Ghosts couldn't care less about their bodies once they've died; they only care to be around the people they loved or hated.

This was the first time in years I wouldn't be going to the cemetery, and it felt really strange. It had become a tradition to go down there, explore the different sections, read all the headstones, and hide from the evil spirits roaming through the night. It was my sanctuary, in a way. But not tonight.

After the photo shoot I headed to Aiden's. I normally walk over, but since it was so cold, my dad gave me a lift on his way to meet Jack's friends. He was just as surprised as my mom that I was going out that night.

"This is a big step for you, buddy," he said. "I'm proud of you."

"I'm dressed as a giant baby to go trick-or-treating, Dad," I said. "I'm not sure this is the best time for you to be proud of me."

He laughed. "Well, you know what I mean."

My dad had worked as a CPA for forever, but after his dad died a few years ago (a traumatic time for the two of us for *very* different reasons), he decided he wanted to be a teacher. Now he teaches math at the local high school. The very same one I'll be attending next year.

"Have a good night, buddy!" he said as I got out of the car in front of Aiden's house.

"Stay away from the scary costumes!" I warned Jack, totally serious. "You don't know who or what will be near them."

Jack's expression melted into a grimace as they

drove away. Ghosts had always scared him, and having me as his big brother was probably his enduring nightmare.

I knocked on the door of Aiden's house and was greeted by his mother, Mrs. Kirkwood. She is the friendliest woman I've ever met but also one of the largest. She took up the entire width of the doorway, and she shrieked when she saw me.

"Aiden told me you were joining in on the fun tonight!" she squealed, wrapping me in a giant hug and pressing me into her soft yet still somehow very firm body. Hugging her fascinated me because it was like hugging a rubbery boulder. When she finally released me, she pushed me back and held me at arm's length so she could look me over. "And that costume, Baylor! So funny! Oh, you four are going to have such a great time tonight! I'm just so excited for you all!"

"Thanks, Mrs. Kirkwood," I said. Kristina laughed next to me, but I didn't acknowledge her. Mrs. Kirkwood could get a little too excited by my gift, so I'd found it was best to pretend like it didn't exist whenever I was around her. "Is everyone here already?"

"You're the first to arrive!" she said giddily, closing the door and leading me to the kitchen, where she

had set out bowls of M&M'S, chips and salsa, and a
gourmet cheese and cracker plate.

Aiden, dressed as a very wide skeleton, was hovering over the bowl of salsa, a handful of chips in his
hand.

"Dude, you actually came!" he said. "I know you
said you would, but I didn't believe it till right now."

"Yeah, I decided to mix it up this year," I said,
grabbing some M&M'S. I looked over his costume
and decided it was okay. I hadn't told him not to
dress as anything negative, and I didn't think a skeleton was too bad. I had one inside of me, after all. It
was really a scientific diagram, I justified to myself. It
totally wasn't a deteriorated corpse. Nope. Nothing
to be afraid of.

"Well, this is going to be awesome," he said. "You
got a bag?"

I frowned because I didn't know what he meant,
and then I slapped my forehead. A bag for the candy!
I hadn't been trick-or-treating in so long that I'd forgotten I needed something for my loot.

"Shoot!" I said. "Totally forgot. Do you have one
I could borrow?"

"Oh, don't worry, Baylor, all the kids use pillow-
cases," Mrs. Kirkwood said as she wandered out of
the kitchen. "I'll grab you one."

"So you're okay, man?" Aiden asked. "Finally gonna face the ghosts out and about tonight?"

"Yeah," I said. "It was time."

"What changed your mind?" He threw a handful of M&M'S into his mouth.

"My mom said something about how this might be the last chance I ever get to trick-or-treat, since we're getting so old."

Mrs. Kirkwood came back in at that moment and wore an expression like I'd just slapped her in the face.

"The last chance?" she said, her lips quivering. "Oh dear. I . . . I didn't even think about—I guess you wouldn't want to trick-or-treat next year as high schoolers. You'll probably have some cool party to go to instead."

"Cool? She knows she's talking to you and Aiden, right?" Kristina chimed in. She was sitting at the kitchen table, looking out the big picture window into the dark woods behind the house.

"Yeah, probably," Aiden said. "We'll barely be able to get away with it tonight."

Kristina snorted. "You're an overgrown toddler, Aiden. You'll be able to trick-or-treat until you're forty!"

The doorbell rang, and Mrs. Kirkwood let in J and Bobby. Bobby, who was dressed as a girl, is one of our really good friends. He's also in band, except he plays the drums. He's one of those guys you can't help but like, and I had a theory that Kristina secretly had a crush on him, not that she could do anything about it. When I looked over at her, she was fixing her hair.

"J" is short for "Janet," and she's one of the scariest people I've ever met. Not scary like a bully, but more like she will look at you and tell you her exact opinion on anything and why she's correct. She'll be going to Harvard or Yale one day; I think it just depends on which one offers her more money. She's not in band with us, but we became friends after Aiden got to know her in Debate Club last year.

"Looking dapper," J said to me as she gave me a hug. She was dressed up as a nurse, but she wasn't wearing a skimpy outfit or even blue scrubs. She had on a long white dress and a floppy white cap, both emblazoned with giant red crosses. Her thick, purple cheetah-print glasses, though, gave her away as a thirteen-year-old girl and not an actual Civil War nurse pestering me to deliver a message.

Aiden was ogling her, and I was trying to catch his eye so he'd remember to close his mouth. He'd harbored a crush on her from the day they met, but he was, in his words, "too fat and goofy" to do anything about it. Instead, he just hung out with her all the time and did everything he could to make her happy, while very much not being her boyfriend. It was depressing to witness.

"Doesn't he realize that she likes him, too?" Kristina said. "I don't understand the logic of blinkers sometimes."

I shrugged but didn't say anything. It was pretty standard communication for the two of us when we were in front of people. She'd make a comment, and I'd find some way to respond. She'd told me that we might be able to communicate with our thoughts one day, but I didn't like the sound of it. What if she accidentally caught some of my private thoughts? There'd be no coming back from that.

"Did they run out of the cute nurse costumes at the store, J?" I asked.

"What are you talking about? I'm Clara Barton."

I blinked, not sure if I was supposed to know what that meant.

"The founder of the American Red Cross," she said, as though it were immensely obvious. Then she pointed at Bobby. "Can you believe this idiot?" He was posing like a Cali girl in his short jean skirt and red top, complete with a stuffed bra, bright-blond wig, and atrocious makeup.

"I thought he was your patient, actually," I joked, and I turned to glare at Aiden. He still hadn't recovered from seeing his crush in her costume, and he needed to get it together. He caught my eye and jumped.

"You guys look great," he managed to choke out. I shook my head while Kristina scoffed from her perch at the table.

"The haul's going to be great this year," Bobby said, his mouth doubled from its normal size thanks to the smeared lipstick covering it. "All the parents who usually hang out on the streets are going to be home, since it's so cold, which means more houses to go to, which means"—he shook his hips excitedly—"more candy for us."

"It's not going to be good candy, though," J said. "They're just going to give us whatever they had lying around, since they didn't have time to run to the store."

"Where," Bobby said, turning to her dramatically, "is your optimism?"

She laughed, and Aiden turned back and forth between them, smiling with a vague look of panic beaming from his eyes.

"Oh, wow, this is like watching a train wreck," Kristina said, exasperated. "Pull it together, Aiden!"

I chuckled, but I didn't know what to do. I had

already given Aiden as much advice as I could. I had dropped hints on his behalf to J. I wasn't sure how to help them, and now it looked like a lost cause. He had wanted to ask her to the Back-to-School Bash in September, but she had been very vocal about wanting to go with a group of friends. When I told him to ask her to the Fall Ball coming up in November, the look on his face suggested that I'd just described a murder scene in gory detail.

"Let's take a picture," J said. She whipped out her cell phone and handed it to Mrs. Kirkwood, who'd been leaning against the fridge the whole time and grinning like a madwoman.

"You all are just so cute," she said under her breath as she squinted at the screen and tapped it aimlessly, while we all pressed together in front of the table. I had specifically positioned myself between Bobby and J so that Aiden was on her other side. "There! I think it worked! I'm not sure, though."

J took back the phone, giggled, and said, "I'm gonna post it right now." She showed it to us, and even though we all looked like fools, the main thing I noticed was a strange light in the corner. Kristina had managed to find her way into the picture in her own special ghost way, and I winked at her. She smiled and nodded.

I wondered, sometimes, what it was like to have only one person to talk to. To be invisible your whole life—could you call what she was experiencing a "life," even?—at the mercy of someone else. I had never asked her, but I wondered why she was the one who'd had to die and I was the one who'd gotten to live. And I wondered if she ever got sad about it. Whether or not she did, on nights like these, when I got to hang out with family and friends and she had to hang out in the corner, silent and unnoticed and effectively non-existent, I felt sad for her.

"This candy sucks!" Bobby yelled as we walked to the next house. "Dum Dums and Tootsie Rolls? I mean, come on, they may as well have opened the door, flipped us off, and spit in our faces."

"I actually like Tootsie Rolls!" J said, her floppy cap bopping up and down with every step she took.

"Me too!" Aiden said quickly, close behind.

"Whatever, you freaks can have them, then," Bobby said. "I'll trade you for the good stuff."

We'd been going for nearly an hour, walking as fast as we could between the houses, since it was only getting colder. Our bags were bulging, and I could tell I had gotten some decent treats. Three houses so far had given out king-size candy bars, which was akin to finding the Holy Grail three separate times.

"Okay, let's turn left down Acorn Road, since that's a good cul-de-sac," Bobby said. "We can hit a bunch of houses really fast."

"Perfect!" said J. "Then maybe we can think about heading back to Aiden's? My legs have only got twenty more minutes, max, before they're going to be classified as medically worthless."

"Are you kidding, J?" Bobby asked. "It's barely been an hour!"

"But we've gone to so many houses!" she said. "How much candy do you need?"

"All of it, J," he crooned. "I want as much as I can get."

She shook her head. "Twenty minutes, then I'm done."

"I'll go back with you, J," Aiden said quietly as Bobby ran ahead. "Don't worry."

J looked up at him and smiled. She couldn't see his face, since it was covered by a black-and-white skeleton mask, but I would have bet an even $1,000 that he was bright red.

When we turned onto Acorn Road, we passed a group of kids in the grade below us. Bobby nodded to them and kept walking, but when I got a look at

their costumes, it was like a lightning bolt had hit
my spine.

One had on a zombie mask with ripped flesh and bloody eyes. Another was dressed in a white shirt covered with blood and tire marks. And still another wore a hockey mask and carried a fake machete.

I had been doing fine all night, focused on hanging with my friends and running from house to house and ignoring everything else, and I had barely noticed a spirit around. But when I saw those costumes, it was so jarring and unexpected that I lost my concentration and an invisible wall crumbled. I was immediately surrounded by spirits, good and demonic alike, and the deafening chatter of a thousand ghosts.

I gasped, and all of a sudden Kristina was in front of me, reminding me to breathe, to shut my eyes and imagine only the good, and to let that image become my reality.

But then she was gone, and my friends were too, and I was all alone on Acorn Road. I looked around at the houses, where all the lights had gone out, yet the decorations glowed an eerie red.

Then, from the gaps in between the houses, a hundred men wearing sheets filed out and charged right at me. They weren't moving their legs; they were floating, their feet angled toward the road like they'd just been hanged.

And there were a hundred pairs of those awful eyes, beady pools of black evil, all illuminated a malicious red from the strange glow, boring into my soul, daggering into my skin.

I turned and ran.

TIP

5

Make sure you can run fast . . . or else.

I RACED DOWN ACORN ROAD, CUT A LEFT, and sprinted like I was competing in the Olympics.

I glanced back and saw the Sheet Men zipping toward me, like I was the magnet and they were pieces of iron, like I was the matador with a giant red cape and they were the angry bulls.

No one else was around. No one was there to help.

If these demons caught up to me and somehow attacked, I'd be all on my own.

I looked ahead. I summoned up all the strength I had and willed my legs to compete with the speed of light. They blurred into pink nothings, moving so fast I couldn't even feel them.

I turned out of Aiden's neighborhood and sprinted down the main road. Not a single car was anywhere in sight.

I looked back again to see how close they were, and immediately I wished I hadn't.

The Sheet Men had taken on a V formation, like a deranged flock of murderous geese, and the leader was mere feet behind me, the white sheet not flapping an inch.

I wasn't fast enough. He'd catch up to me at any second. I could feel the energy around me changing, and everything becoming hazy. I could sense that he was about to take over my soul and enlist me into his sheet-wearing army. I knew it was over.

Then, with an almighty bang, Kristina materialized in front of me, shimmering into my view as sparks of blue rained down around her. That red glow suddenly vanished, and after I skidded to a stop, I turned to see all the Sheet Men had gone too.

Except now I was in the middle of a busy road, and a truck was speeding right for me.

"Look out!" Kristina cried. She lunged for me, blasting me to the side of the road in another tornado of blue sparks. I rolled into a cold, muddy

ditch, tumbling several feet down into a swampy
crevasse.

Once I stopped rolling, I lay there for a second,
panting hard and shallow, my pink pajamas now covered in mud and bits of grass.

"Baylor," Kristina said, "are you okay? Are you hurt?"

I didn't respond because I hadn't attempted to
move any part of my body. The shock of the last
couple minutes was still too great. I couldn't feel
anything.

"Baylor, say something!"

I squeezed my eyelids together, then looked over
at her figure, which was still glowing blue, and said,
"Did you see how fast I ran?"

"Baylor! You almost just got killed!"

"I guess you're not a very good guardian angel,
then," I said, closing my eyes again, digging my head
deeper into the mud.

"You disappeared from my sight! I had no idea
where you'd gone, or how. It's never happened before."

"Well, that's comforting," I mumbled.

"I had to cross to the Beyond and get one of my
guides to help me break whatever trance you were under."

"That explains the blue," I said, waving my hand
in a figure-eight pattern over her body. The shimmer
had nearly faded away.

"Yes," she said stiffly. "I don't have that sort of power yet."

"One day," I said. I raised my torso, resting on my elbows to look around. No one had pulled over to check on me. My friends were probably still on Acorn Road, wondering how I'd vanished. I didn't have the energy to find them and make up some lie. "Let's go to the cemetery."

She cocked her head at me, but she nodded. Slowly I rose from the ground and tried to brush myself off, but a thick layer of mud and leaves stuck to my hand. I shook it off and started walking.

As we made our way down the road, I couldn't quite keep the spirits tuned out. It was just like listening to the radio and having static come in and disrupt a song. Every few seconds I'd suddenly see ghosts speeding down the highway at sixty miles an hour, surrounding the cars, and then they'd disappear.

The cemetery was only a ten-minute walk, but in my current state it took double that time. We walked in silence. Once we'd reached Woodland Cemetery, I threw myself over the fence that divided it from the road, and landed on the soft grass with a gentle thud.

I let out a big breath as a feeling of relief washed over me. I was in my sanctuary, and I felt safe. It didn't matter that the spirits kept flickering in and out. I was now in the one place where none of them would be.

I walked aimlessly for a little bit, passing by several unfamiliar stones, until I finally spotted the big spruce tree next to the little road that cut through the cemetery.

From there I followed the road for a bit, looking for the tombstone topped by a cherubic angel with a chipped wing. Turning left, I counted seven markers until I got to the one I wanted.

When I was eleven, one of my classmates died in a horrific car accident, the kind where they had to bring in dental records to identify the bodies. His name was Tommy Thorne, and though he wasn't a good friend of mine, he was still someone I had seen nearly every day for almost my entire life.

I got to know him better after he died, after passing on a couple of messages to Tommy's father, from both his son and his wife. Since then, whenever I visited the cemetery, I always found myself back at his grave.

The dark-gray stone was etched with his name, the words BELOVED SON underneath. I had traced my fingers through those letters so many times. It was fascinating to me that he had been in the physical world, eating a bowl of cereal for breakfast and then picking out his favorite shirt to wear for the trip to the mall with his mom, not suspecting a thing, totally unaware that his life was going to end. One second he was here, and the next he was there, on the other side, in the place where only I could still see him.

Tonight I wasn't going to say hi. I didn't want to talk to anyone except for Kristina. But I made sure to send over some positive vibes through the mental barrier that separated my sanity from all the roaming souls and spirits, just to let him know I was thinking of him.

I had other things on my mind, though. Bigger, scarier things.

Namely, the fact that my sister kept being forced away by a silent, creepy man covered in a white sheet who had apparently recruited many more demons to help him . . . help him what? Kill me? Attack me? Scare me? Send me a message?

I had no idea why any of it was happening. A simple note or a few quick words would have been a tremendous help, but I got nothing. So I sat there in my dirty Halloween costume, my back against Tommy's grave, and wondered aloud to Kristina all those thoughts.

"It's so random," I said. "I have nothing to go on. It's like I'm being attacked for no reason."

Kristina nodded. "It doesn't make sense."

"Didn't you say my 'protection' had been amped up? What happened?"

"If there was really a hundred of them chasing after you, the extra protection probably didn't help much. These are evil beings, Baylor. They're infiltrating our defenses in ways I can't understand, and it definitely doesn't help that I can't get a look at them to see what we're dealing with."

"Then I need to fight back, Kristina," I said. "What can I do?"

She stared at me for several seconds and began to pace.

"First things first, you need to begin surrounding yourself with light every hour. Twice a day clearly isn't enough. Carry a candle and set an alarm to remember to light it. We'll keep several candles lit at night, too."

"Great. More candles. Got it," I said, picking at the grass. "I'm not going to lie, Kristina, I'm getting a lit bit tired of having to rely on freaking candles. There's got to be a more powerful weapon I can use, maybe something that's actually a weapon and not what kids blow out on their birthdays after making a wish that won't come true."

She stopped moving and shot me a look. "Candles are fine for now," she said tersely.

"So there is something else!" My eyes narrowed into slits. "You've been keeping it from me!"

"You know the drill, Baylor," she said, pacing again. "We're not ready yet."

I rolled my eyes. Of course.

"Plus, I want to see if the disturbances will continue once Halloween is over."

It was a good point. In just a few hours the costumes would be peeled off and tossed away by everyone in the city, and the negative energy would begin to fade—not all at once, of course, but it wouldn't be maxing out at its current wattage.

"So we'll wait," I said. "I'll layer myself with plenty of light, and we'll hope that the visits stop now that this terrible day is ending."

"I think that'll do for now," she said, nodding. "And if it doesn't, we'll come up with a plan."

I smiled grimly. "Tiki torches?"

A bit later I called my mom and asked her to come pick me up at the cemetery. When she arrived, she got out of her car and ran over to me, looking frantic. She squeezed my face and then sort of attempted a hug, but after she saw how dirty I was, it turned into more of a pat on the back.

"What happened to you?" she asked, shaking mud off her hand.

"It's kind of a long story," I said. "I'll tell you

back at the house so Dad can hear it too."

I spent most of the ride home deflecting concerned texts from Aiden. He wasn't mad or anything, just really confused, since I'd dropped my bag of candy and then disappeared without anyone noticing. He said he'd bring the candy to me on Monday, but he couldn't guarantee there'd be much left, because Mrs. Kirkwood thoroughly enjoyed the spoils of Halloween.

Mom and Dad were not happy once I relayed all the events of the last couple of days.

"That thing was in our house and you didn't bother to mention it until now?" my mom shrieked. She had begun chopping random vegetables midway through the story, even though it was nearly eleven o'clock at night. She'd plowed through two onions, a red bell pepper, and a lumpy sweet potato by the time I finished.

"I didn't know the Sheet Man was going to return," I said. "I thought it was a one-time visitation."

"One-time visitation," she scoffed under her breath. "Till the thing came back with a hundred of his dead little demon friends and made you almost get hit by a semitruck."

My dad sat across from me at the table, his chin

pushed back into his neck, creating four additional chins. He was looking at his hands, and I wasn't sure if he'd heard a word I'd said.

"It was either the truck or a hundred Sheet Men getting their wispy hands on you," Kristina said from her spot at the head of the table. She'd been reminding me of details to add in.

"That's true," I mumbled.

"What'd she say?" Dad asked, looking up suddenly.

"She said it was better to nearly get hit by a truck than to have a hundred of those things finally catch up to me."

My mom threw down her knife, which clanged violently onto the counter, and marched over to me.

"Kristina, I don't know where you are, but you need to do something, okay?" my mom sputtered. "You need to make sure this can't happen again." She looked at me, then quickly turned to stare out the window into the blackness, but not so quickly that I couldn't see the tears welling up. "I've already lost you," she said, her voice cracking. "I can't lose another one."

Kristina's mouth hung open slightly. I had never seen her speechless before. She rose from the table and walked over to Mom. She tried to hug her, but as always, her body just sort of sank in, making them look like Siamese twins.

My mom shivered violently and her shoulders jerked back. "I've never gotten the chills that bad before!"

"Kristina just hugged you," I said.

She shot me a strange look, a mixture of sadness and panic, then hurried back to her cutting board and resumed her violent chopping.

"Well, this has been a stranger night than usual," I said after another minute of silence. Part of me wondered if I should have just kept all this to myself. The stress of hearing this story would do no favors for my dad's rapidly graying hair.

My dad nodded, throwing his hands open. "I don't know what to say, Baylor. I feel so helpless. If those guys wearing sheets were real people, I'd say forget the police and just hunt them down myself. But in this situation . . . I don't know what to do."

"We light candles," I said, smiling sarcastically at Kristina, who stuck her tongue out at me. "And we stay positive."

He attempted to smile, but it resembled that same sort of pained, teeth-baring grimace that he'd worn after finishing his first marathon a couple of years ago. He stood, walked to the hall closet, and pulled out the duffel bag of candles we had stockpiled inside.

"Let's get to work."

We finished protecting the house in less than ten minutes, and afterward I went up to bed while my mom was throwing all the ingredients into a pot to make some veggie chili.

"Might as well," she said. "I won't be sleeping tonight anyway."

In the bathroom I finally peeled off my dirty pink costume and looked at myself in the mirror. Man, I was gross. My entire face was flecked with mud and grass, and everything else ached from the extensive tumbling I'd done off the side of the road.

I took what must have been a thirty-minute shower and then collapsed into my bed.

"Good night, Baylor," said Kristina, who was lit up by the glow of the ten massive candles I'd placed around my room earlier.

"Good night, Kristina," I said, yawning. "Thanks for your help tonight."

"Of course," she said. She hesitated a moment. "I just wanted to say, before I go for the night, that I'm sorry I didn't protect you better."

"It's not your fault," I said, my eyes closed. I secretly wished she'd go.

"I know," she said. "But I still feel like I let you down."

"You didn't," I said lightly, peeking my eyes open.
"You did your best."

She looked odd, though, and if I hadn't been so tired, I would have pressed her on the subject. But before I knew it, she'd vanished, and I passed out not five seconds later.

6

Tubas may cause bodily harm. Proceed with caution.

I SPENT ALL SUNDAY IN BED, MY BODY POSI-
tively on fire from the tumble the night before, but
between the frequent bowls of veggie chili delivered
by my mother and the hours of TV that I mindlessly
watched, I began to feel somewhat better.

Monday, however, was dreadful. I could barely
walk, and I'd completely forgotten about a science
quiz I needed to study for.

"What kind of a ridiculous jerk gives a quiz the
Monday after Halloween weekend?" I mumbled
to Kristina on my way to the next class. "And you

wouldn't even help me out with any of the answers. I
bombed that so bad."

"You know I can't help you, Baylor!" Kristina said.
"We've been over this maybe a million times."

"It wouldn't hurt anyone to help me out a little bit."

"That's what you think," she said ominously.

I ignored her comment and marched on, somehow
getting through the day and looking forward to band
practice. I thought about skipping it, but since I'd
missed Thursday, I felt like I had to go.

I'd started playing the tuba on a whim a few years
ago. I had tried out for soccer because I liked how
much I got to run, but I quit during my first game.
There were far too many ghosts on the field, and I
could barely tell who was a player and who was dead.
Twenty minutes in I stomped off the field and told
my parents I couldn't play anymore.

Playing the tuba, on the other hand, has become
my saving grace. Whereas running around in soccer
allowed my mind to be too receptive to all the spirits
around me, playing the tuba forces me to concentrate
on the music. The sound helps block out all the chatter. After a few minutes of staring at sheet music,
I almost transform into someone who can't talk to
dead people. I'd never admit this to Kristina, but it's
nice to feel truly alone, even if it's only for a little bit.

Four years later, and I'm still playing the tuba. I've learned to play the guitar and the piano, too, but I prefer the tuba. There's something about wrapping that instrument around my body and blasting music out of it that makes me feel like I'm in my own little world with no one to bother me.

The band instructor, Mr. Gilbert, was a short man with long, curly red hair. He wore a tie every single day, and today it was decked out in little Snoopy drawings.

"Looking good, Mr. G.," I said as I limped into the giant room. There were a bunch of skylights that lined the ceiling, casting a dull, wintry light over the room, and flimsy blue soundproofing material covered every wall.

"Glad to see you're feeling better, Baylor," he said, "though that limp doesn't look too great."

"Took a nasty spill on Halloween," I said. "Collecting free candy is hard work."

He raised an eyebrow at me. "Children," he said, shaking his head and smiling.

I got my tuba from the instrument closet and said hey to Aiden before taking my place in the semicircle of chairs. He'd given me the surprisingly full bag of Halloween candy at lunch.

"I had to hide it from my mom in my dirty-clothes

hamper," he'd said. "You know how she gets." I'd searched for some Twix while trying not to think about my candy languishing next to Aiden's filthy underwear for two days.

As he unpacked another pepperoni-and-mustard sandwich, he'd asked, "So where'd you disappear to, anyway? Why'd you drop all your candy?"

I'd sort of frowned at him and said, "Believe me, Aiden, you do *not* want to know." He'd widened his eyes and didn't ask anything else about it.

Today we were prepping for the parade that would take place downtown on Main Street the weekend before Thanksgiving. We'd be near the end of the parade, and Mr. G. felt confident that tackling a Christmas medley would set the mood for the holiday season.

"A classic medley!" he said. "Something we've never done before but that's been done to death by everyone else in America."

"Then why are we doing it, if it's been done before?" asked one of the saxophonists.

"Because we live in Keene, New Hampshire," he said slowly. "Our town loves anything festive."

It was true. Our town was infamous for its huge pumpkin festival, trying to break a Guinness world record for the most jack-o'-lanterns lit at once, and at Christmastime the downtown square transformed into a majestic, brightly lit wonderland.

Mr. G. passed out the sheet music and asked us to play through everything once so he could gauge what needed the most work. We started with a rough rendition of "Jingle Bells," followed by "The Little Drummer Boy," and finally finished with an interesting mash-up of "Silent Night" and "All I Want for Christmas Is You."

We sounded so bad I wasn't sure what Mr. G. would think needed the most fine-tuning, and he looked just as perplexed. He'd winced with every wrong note and disharmonious chord, which meant his flowing hair had whipped around nearly nonstop for ten minutes.

He decided to start with the mash-up: If it wasn't going to work, he wanted to know fairly early so that we could practice something entirely different.

After running through it four times, I started to get a little bored. Considering "Silent Night" was a peaceful, almost relaxing song, the tuba didn't have much of a place. I began to sing the lyrics in my head, closing my eyes and letting the positive energy of the Christmas music overcome me. Christmas was the one time of year when I never had any trouble with ghosts.

Silent night! Holy night!
All is calm, all is bright
Round yon Virgin Mother and Child.
Holy Infant, so tender and mild,
Sleep in heavenly peace,
Sleep in heavenly peace.

When we had to stop and do it a fifth time, I sighed and looked at Aiden, who was visibly sweating. He was in the opposite situation from me: The flute was prominently featured.

By now even I could tell the mash-up wasn't going to work. How on earth would Mariah Carey lyrics fit in there?

"One, two, three . . . ," Mr. G. called out, and I reclined back, closed my eyes, and began to recite the lyrics in my head once more.

Silent night! Holy night!
All is calm . . .

The music stopped all at once. I opened my eyes to see what had happened, but I was alone in the room.

Except I wasn't alone—he was there.

The Sheet Man was standing in the middle of the semicircle, staring at me. He hadn't brought his cronies this time. It was just him and me, and by this point I'd had enough.

"What do you want?" I said, standing up with my tuba. "Say something or stop bothering me."

He didn't say a word, but the sheet, which had remained so still before, began to whip violently, like a tornado had just entered the room. It raised higher a bit, and for the first time I caught a good glimpse of his shoes: some kind of brown leather with an odd, shiny buckle on top.

I couldn't see them for more than a second or two, though, because once that nonexistent wind started blowing, I began to feel light-headed. So light-headed that I began to question how I was still standing, how I had gotten to this room, how I was still alive even.

It felt like he was sucking all the energy out of me.

"Stop," I said, clasping my tuba for support, forgetting I was the one supporting it in the first place. "Stop!"

It did stop, and I found myself swaying back in the middle of the band room full of my friends, all of whom had stopped playing and were turned my way, their mouths agape in horror. But it was too late. It felt like all the blood had left my body, and before I could do anything else, I went crashing to the floor.

Ghosts, just like living people, can be quite rude.

DURING THOSE FIRST CONFUSED SECONDS after I came to, I had no idea where I was, what the time was, why there was a huge crowd of people around me, and why my head hurt so much.

"Finally, he's up," said a squat woman to my left. She had brown hair that was twisted into a bun on her head, and she looked at me like she was scolding a naughty child. "We've been waiting for hours."

"What took so long?" said a gruff bald man in a black biker vest, tattoos covering his bare arms. "It was just a tuba."

"Move over!" a familiar voice said. "Get out of the way!"

Kristina emerged from behind a large, frowning woman who was wearing a muumuu.

"Baylor!" she said. "How's your head?"

"Not good," I said, trying to lift my arm from the stiff hospital bed but getting caught in a jungle of wires.

"Your head is covered with electrodes," she said. "Monitoring for a concussion."

"Great," I moaned. "Where are Mom and Dad?"

"Outside talking to the doctor."

"Never mind your parents, they're fine," said the first woman. "I need you to tell my daughter that her husband is a scumbag. She's right down the hall."

"Enough with this demon dung!" Kristina said, enraged. She turned and pointed her finger at the woman.

"Oh no," the woman said as a blue wave of light surrounded her body before she vanished.

"Wow," I said. "I didn't know you could do that."

"Neither did we," said the bald biker guy, taking a step back.

"I've been developing some new tricks with my spirit guides the last few days," Kristina said, flexing her fingers. "That felt weird."

"How so?" I asked. It was funny to hear Kristina describe things because she couldn't actually touch anything in the physical world and had no true reference.

"It felt hot, like whenever you get into the car in the summer and all you do is shift around and complain about how it takes forever to cool down."

"I don't do that!"

"My goal is to find this Sheet Man who keeps making an appearance and zap him into the next universe," she said, ignoring my denial.

"Did you just zap that woman into some weird universe?" I asked.

"No, I just made her go away," she said, shrugging. "She was being rude."

"Does this mean he's not going to deliver messages right now?" asked the woman in the muumuu.

"Obviously," Kristina snapped. "How could he? He's confined to his bed."

"He could call a nurse and have her deliver the messages room to room."

The crowd chimed in with their approval.

"That works!"

"He's not doing anything else!"

"My son needs to know he's dating a thief!"

"No!" Kristina said firmly. "The only reason

he can see you right now is because he can't focus enough to tune you out. Just because he's in the hospital doesn't mean he's your slave."

"It would be a nice thing, helping us," said the tattooed man.

"You know what would be really nice?" Kristina said, her voice seeped with venom. "It would be so nice if all of you would leave the room and come back at a more appropriate time. Our parents are coming back in a few seconds anyway."

"This isn't fair."

"Our families need to hear these things. That's what he's here for."

"He's seriously dating a thief! She steals raw meats from the grocery store! Who does that?"

"I never said I wouldn't help you," I said as they all backed out of the room in one smooth motion, like a vacuum was sucking them out. I wasn't sure if that was part of Kristina's new powers or if it was of their own accord. "I'm just not going to right now."

As the last spirits groaned their way out of the room, I noticed a doctor standing near the door, my parents next to him. He was probably in his late thirties, and he didn't look happy at all.

"You can't be serious," he said, turning to my parents. "I'm supposed to listen to him talk to an empty room for minutes on end and accept that nothing is wrong with his brain? You are both out of your minds."

"He does this all the time," my dad said in the same light, singsong voice he used with Ella. "It's perfectly normal."

"Talks to ghosts," the doctor mumbled, writing something on my chart. "Outrageous. The kid is hallucinating."

I shot a look at Kristina, and a moment later two old women were standing next to her.

"Thank you for letting us back in," the first one said. She was tall and had that long silver hair only a few old ladies can really pull off, though I wasn't so sure she was one of them.

"Dean's going through a hard time right now," the second one said. Her hair was the correct length, and she had a huge, gleaming smile that would have made me smile if the nerves in my face hadn't been screaming in agony right then. "His brother, Dillon, has a rare form of lung cancer. He only started smoking after he saw Dean do it when they were younger, but Dillon could never kick the habit after Dean did."

"He needs to let go of his guilt!" the one with long hair said. "Dillon is a grown man and made his choices. Dean didn't force a cigarette into his brother's mouth the first time he tried it, and he didn't force-feed every single one to him for twenty years, either."

I nodded to each of them and said, "Thank you," which made the doctor scoff and throw up his hands.

"This is ridiculous," he said.

"Uh, Dean? Can I call you Dean?" I asked, not leaving him any time to answer. "It's what your grandmas called you."

His eyes widened. "My grandmas?"

"They know you're in a bad place because of Dillon's cancer, but they want you to let go of the guilt associated with it."

He dropped the chart. "Who did you hear talking about this? Was it Marta? I'm going to have her fired. I knew I couldn't trust her."

"No! Don't fire Marta, I don't even know who that is," I said. "Your grandmas are standing right there." I pointed to the space to my left, next to a silver cart. He looked over, but of course he saw nothing.

"He was always so stubborn," the short-haired grandma said, laughing.

"I'll keep trying," I said under my breath. "Dean, Dillon may have lung cancer, but you didn't give it to him. You're not responsible for it."

"Why are you playing this trick on me?" the doctor

said. I'm sure his aura was bloodred with fury. "This
is a very personal subject."

"I'm not tricking you at all. One of your grand-mas has long hair and talks with a very proper accent, almost like she's British, but I know she's not. The other one has short hair and doesn't stop smiling. She's also way shorter than the other one."

Dean's hands started shaking as he searched the empty space where they stood beaming at him.

"Mention the little Easter chick he got as a child that lasted maybe five minutes before the dog got it," the long-haired grandma said. "That should do the trick."

Once I repeated that back to Dean, he left the room, still looking incredibly annoyed, and said he would return in a few minutes. The grandmas fol-lowed him out.

"Well, that was awkward," my mom said, plopping into the armchair next to my bed. "We mentioned to him that you might do that, just so he wouldn't think there was anything wrong with you if you started, you know, communicating with . . . them."

My dad wasn't looking at me because he was wiping away tears from his eyes. Ever since his father crossed over, he became emotional whenever he witnessed me delivering a message of any kind.

"What happened, Baylor?" my mom said, massaging

my right hand. "You've never passed out like that before. Were you feeling sick?" She spoke in a cheerful voice that was so obviously fake I couldn't let her continue for a second longer.

"It was the Sheet Man," I said. "He made an appearance during band practice, and this time I stood up to him. Except that after I stood up, I lost all my energy and the tuba fell on me. I knew I should have taken up the flute."

I grimaced at the memory.

"Oh my God," she said, her smile melting, the cheerful tone eliminated. "I knew it."

"The candles didn't work?" Dad asked.

"I guess not," I said. "Kristina is even learning some new powers, and with all that, he still got through to me."

"Isn't there a ghost police or something that can help you?" Mom's voice was raised, exasperated. "This guy needs to leave you alone! Oh God, I don't ever want to die, it's just chaos over there, Baylor."

"Calm down," I said. "If he wanted to hurt me, he would have already."

"Baylor, do you not see where you are right now?" she asked, her voice going up to an unsustainable octave. "You're lying in a hospital bed with your head all wrapped up!"

"Okay, maybe that wasn't the best choice of words," I said, "but I sort of caused this on my own."

"It's working," she said, panicked, turning to my dad. "That thing, it's working its evil powers on him already. He's getting Stockholm syndrome, but for ghosts! Stocksoul syndrome!" She turned back to me, her eyes moving like crazy over my face. "Snap out of it, Baylor!" She snapped both of her hands in my face. "That thing is dangerous! It wants to hurt you."

Kristina started laughing hysterically, and even I had to focus really hard to keep my mouth from twitching.

"Mom, you're overreacting," I said. "I promise you, I don't have Stocksoul syndrome. I'm just trying to figure out what's going on."

The concern remained in her eyes.

"I'll be watching you like a hawk, Baylor Bosco," she said. "Any sign of any of the sheet craziness, and I'm getting the holy water out."

8

Not all healing messages are created equal.

DOCTOR DEAN EVENTUALLY RECOVERED and came back into the room. He made no mention of my messages, but he didn't keep calling me crazy, either, so I guessed he believed me. He told me I had to stay overnight for observation, but that I was most likely fine. I just got my "bell rung" really good, as he said, causing my father to interject with, "More like he got his tuba blown." No one laughed.

I managed to persuade my mom not to spend the night. At first she flat-out refused to listen to me, saying the evil spirits were making me say that and it was all the more reason for her to stay, but I managed to turn that thinking around on her, saying that the hospital was filled with spirits that would play tricks on her, keep her up all night, and make her think she was going insane.

I knew I'd hit the nail on the head when I said the word "insane," because her eyes got really wide and it was clear she was starting to feel that way. She'd been pacing around the room nonstop and blurting out nonsensical things about sheets, and I made a pact with myself not to mention the Sheet Man to her anymore. The fewer details, the better.

It took a while, but she finally agreed to leave with my dad, which was exactly what I wanted, because Kristina and I needed time to talk.

"Kristina, he was wearing shoes," I said once they'd left. I'd decided to leave out that detail earlier in case my mom ran home and lit all our shoes on fire. "He showed them to me in the band room. They looked nice. Brown, leather, had some sort of fancy buckle on top of each one."

"It had shoes on?" she said incredulously. "Wow. I've never heard of a demon that wears brown loafers."

"That's the thing, Kristina: How do we know it's a demon? What if it's something else? What if it's someone who needs help?"

"Baylor," she said slowly, as if I were the dumbest person on Earth. "I understand that you think seeing shoes is a good thing in this situation, but let me remind you that neither I nor my spirit guides can control this thing. We can't be in the same space as it. I don't care if it was wearing gold shoes and dancing to jazz music, if I can't be in the same space as it, that's bad. Very bad."

I swallowed. "All right. They're evil shoes, then."

She nodded. "Good twin."

But in the back of my mind I still thought I was right.

"Aiden was here with his mom, by the way," Kristina said. "You were still passed out, so Mom and Dad told them to go home, because they didn't know how long it would be before you woke up." She eyed me with a sly grin. "Though I think the real reason was that Mrs. Kirkwood was sobbing uncontrollably and making everyone feel uncomfortable."

I chuckled and grabbed my phone. Twenty-seven texts from Aiden, three from J, one from Bobby, and a few more from some other friends. Aiden's were mainly a steady stream of panicked thoughts.

AIDEN: ARE YOU OK!?!?!?!?!?!?!?!?!

AIDEN: That tuba was SO heavy!

**AIDEN: Mom's baking everything for you.
Jack's not allergic to peanuts anymore, right?**

**AIDEN: Can't wait to reenact Mr. G's reaction to
your fall!**

I texted back.

**BAYLOR: Finally awake. Have to spend night
at hospital. Getting monitored for a concussion.
Hopefully my tuba career isn't over.**

Aiden responded almost immediately, first with a
million exclamation points, then with

**AIDEN: Glad you're alive!! Eating mom's cookies,
really good!**

"Should we go deliver some messages?" I asked, setting my phone down. "Might as well. If there's one
place to offer some healing guidance, I guess it's here."

"Okay, but you're not telling that guy that his girl-
friend is a thief."

"She is, though!" that same earnest voice echoed

yet again. The man who'd said it materialized before us. He had a case of male-pattern baldness so severe that even a trip to the Beyond couldn't fix it. "He's thinking about marrying her, but it's only a matter of time before that klepto gets caught with five pounds of raw chicken stuffed in her underwear."

I frowned. "Well, okay, maybe I'll just talk to him first and feel out the situation."

Kristina shook her head. "That isn't a healing message, Baylor, you don't need to pass it on."

"Kristina, we're in a hospital filled with hundreds of sick people and all their dead relatives, and I can't tune them out right now. If I get picky about which messages to deliver, we're going to have a bunch of annoying ghosts on our hands, and you're going to be zapping them away all night with your new blue magic."

"I wish I could sigh," she said, shaking her head. "This would have been the perfect time for one."

The next couple of hours were the most hectic I'd ever experienced. Ghosts swarmed me: I was a flame, and they were moths.

I had to stop saying my introductory sentence to people because I had too many messages to deliver. Floor after floor, room after room, person after

person, I was chased by loved ones and spouted off
as many messages as I could breathe, each one as
nonsensical as the next, but filled with meaning for
the receiver.

"Ma'am, don't go visit her, your husband says she's
not worth your time, especially since you're in the
hospital and it could be limited."

"She was right about the first one, sir. I don't know
who the 'she' is or what the 'one' is, though—sorry,
that's all your sister told me to say."

"You need to make the trip. Huh? Oh, sorry, you
need to make the trip soon, like tomorrow. I know
you're in the hospital. Sorry, I'm just delivering the
message from your mom."

"I'm supposed to mention a green duck to you.
That's all they want me to say. I know it's weird, but
your grandparents are the ones who said it, not me."

Toward the end of my time walking the halls, the
messages were thinning out, so I was able to stop
and chat a little bit more. As I passed by one room,
I noticed a little boy staring intensely at the woman
resting on the hospital bed.

I walked in slowly and knelt down next to him.

"Hey there, buddy," I said. "My name's Baylor,
and if you want to say something to your grandma, I
can help you out."

He turned to me, his eyes full of concern. "How'd you know she's my grandma?"

That was a tough question for me to answer. The ghosts don't need to tell me. Sort of like how Kristina can show me auras, I can sense the energy running between the loved ones. I can tell right away what sort of relationship people shared, and continue to share.

"What's your name?" I asked.

"Louie."

"Well, Louie, I guess I just know certain things," I said.

"Can I help you with something?" the woman in the bed asked. She had a shock of tidy white hair, which didn't move an inch as she leaned over the side of her bed to watch me.

"Hi there," I said, standing up. "My name is Baylor Bosco, and I can communicate with people who've crossed over."

"You *what?*" Her voice quivered.

"Um, I can talk to dead people."

She shook her head, her mouth slightly open. "My drugs are really messing with my head right now." She shut her eyes tight, clenching her face together like she was bracing for a punch. Then she opened them again, looking disappointed to see me still standing there.

"Grandma's funny," Louie said, smiling sadly.

I smiled at him and looked back at his grandma, whose face had contorted into a pained expression. "I'm too afraid to ask why you keep looking down at that one spot."

"What's your name, ma'am?"

"Elmira," she said. "Elmira Ashworth."

"Elmira, your grandson Louie is here." He'd walked to the bed and peered over the foot of it, his eyes just barely peeking over the edge. "He's wearing a blue baseball hat and uniform. All that's missing is a glove."

She didn't say anything. She just looked at me, terrified.

"Louie, do you want me to tell your grandma anything?"

He seemed just as upset as his grandma was. I bent down again to talk to him quietly.

"Hey, buddy, it's okay," I said. "You don't have to say anything if you don't want to."

Elmira clenched her covers. "He doesn't want to talk to me," she said in a small, tense voice. "He's mad at me."

Louie nodded.

"Uhh," I said awkwardly. "Yeah, he's nodding."

She reached for the tissue box on the Formica

table next to her bed, speaking in a calm, controlled voice that made me think she was seconds away from totally losing it. "It's my fault he's dead. I'm such a careful driver. I always check the road three times to make sure everything's clear before I go at a green light. And that day . . . this guy came out of nowhere."

"That's not why I'm mad," Louie said quickly.

"He's not mad about that," I said just as quickly, hoping to staunch her crying.

"He's not?" she asked, horrified. "What else is there?"

"Tell her I'm mad that she stopped going to the park. I'm mad that she stopped playing cards with her friends and going dancing. I'm mad that a nice old man asked her to dinner last month and she said no." He turned to me, his eyes bulging. "I'm mad that she's using me as an excuse to stop living."

I paused for a moment, trying to figure out if there was a way to deliver his message that wouldn't totally crush her soul. Maybe if I just sounded casual enough . . .

If I thought I was phrasing my words gently, Elmira's reaction immediately tipped me off that I didn't do a good enough job. She wailed, profusely, for ten minutes, doing her best impression of a hungry newborn baby. Four times I had to turn the nurses away with some vague excuse.

"This is the worst message I've ever given," I said to Kristina out of the corner of my mouth.

"Just wait," Kristina said.

Louie's anger had reconstituted itself as concern after he saw his grandma's reaction, and he'd climbed into bed next to her. Several times she'd massaged the spot on her arm where his head was touching.

Finally, once her sobs had sputtered out, she caught her breath and looked at me.

"Where is he?" she said. "I want to look at him for a moment. Or I want him to look right at me."

"He's right next to you," I said. "He's the reason why your arm's been tingling."

She gasped. "Is that so?"

She looked down at the nothing beside her, the nothing that used to be her everything, and she smiled.

"Louie, I'm sorry," she said. "You're right. I've been dishonoring your memory by sulking at home for the last year. This guilt, though, it's just . . . so unlike anything I've felt. I can't escape it."

"Tell her it wasn't her fault. She was taking me to get ice cream at the park that day. She's the best grandma ever."

When I repeated his words, Elmira smiled, still trying to spot her grandson next to her. "It was going to be such a good day. You and your orangesicles."

"You need to have more of those good days, Grandma! Don't think of me and be sad. Think of me and be happy about all the memories we made."

As I said that to her, she seemed in danger of howling again, but she held it together.

"I love you," Louie said. And with his message delivered, he faded away.

"He's gone," I said. "But the last thing he said was 'I love you.'"

"I know," she said. "I could feel it."

"Well, that was intense," I said. "Sorry, I didn't mean to upset you. That happens sometimes with these messages."

"No, no, are you kidding?" she said. "Come here and give me a hug, Baylor Bosco."

As I hugged Elmira, a horrible sensation came over me and, like I'd touched a hot pan, I shot away from her, a distant hiss penetrating my ears.

"Did you hear that?" I asked Kristina.

Eyebrows raised, she shook her head no.

"Hear what?" Elmira asked.

"I just heard and felt something . . . odd," I said. "Odd" was far too positive a word, but I didn't want to upset her again. "It was just a whisper, though. It said, 'You left me,' and it made me want to vomit."

That was all it took for the color and joy she'd just gained to drain from her face. She started fidgeting with a ring on her right middle finger.

"Do you know who that was?" I asked.

"I think you'd better go," she said icily, staring at the beige curtain.

"Elmira, who was that?"

"Someone . . . from a long time ago."

"Someone bad?"

She stiffened but didn't say anything else, so I apologized and left the room.

"What was that?" I asked, walking quickly back to my room.

"I didn't hear or feel anything, Baylor," Kristina said. She sounded worried, and when Kristina worries, I panic.

"Kristina, whatever it was, it was bad. How did an evil spirit just communicate with me?"

"I don't know."

"The Sheet Man just stares at me with his weird black eyes, but he never says anything, and he never actually touched me. But whatever just happened, that was new. And it's not good, especially since Halloween's over." We entered my room and I shut the door. "It's not just the Sheet Man anymore. They're all starting to break the barrier, aren't they?"

She pursed her lips. "That's the last straw. Tonight I'm bringing in reinforcements."

9

Not all ghosts
stick around. ☹

AS IF I WEREN'T ALREADY FREAKED OUT
enough, the next morning I woke up to discover two
horrible things.

First, I didn't have a candle. Candles weren't
allowed in hospitals, according to some nurse with
an attitude problem, because they were a fire hazard.

"Not having a candle is a hazard to my life," I
replied. "Do you want me to die? You need to find
me a candle right now."

"You're not getting a candle," she said flatly, and
walked out.

Second, Kristina was nowhere to be found. When I go to bed, she goes somewhere in the Beyond to learn, to update her spirit guides, to ask for advice, to socialize (I assume), and essentially to become a better ghost, all while loosely monitoring my dreams and making sure no one's attacking me in my sleep.

When I wake up, she's always there. It was completely and incontrovertibly unlike her to be absent.

Except for that brief period when she was gone for a while.

Just before I turned eight, I woke up early one day to find my grandpa sitting at the kitchen table. He lived out of town, and my parents hadn't told me he was visiting from Ohio. I ran over to him in my Ninja Turtle pajamas and gave him the biggest hug I knew how.

At least, I tried to hug him. Ghosts may not be transparent, but they're definitely not solid.

"Hey there, Baylor, my buddy boy," he said, kneeling down. "Things are a bit different now, huh?"

I backed away, not sure what to do or how to react. I looked at Kristina, who seemed just as confused. Until then I'd never interacted with anyone on the other side except for Kristina, and as far as I knew, Kristina hadn't either.

Grandpa smiled, but in a strained way that looked

more like a frown.

"You don't need to be sad or scared, Baylor. It's just me."

In my head I definitely wasn't sad or scared. I'd been putting things together. Grandpa had lived far away when he was alive, but now he was dead. And I could communicate with ghosts. So that meant I'd get to see him all the time now. This was great news!

I told him so and then said, "I'm hungry. Want to watch me eat breakfast?"

Grandpa definitely wasn't reacting the way I'd expected. He looked heartbroken. "I . . . I came to say good-bye, kiddo," he said. "I just want you to know how much I love you. And your parents and brother, too."

"Huh?"

"And there's something else, too." He reached out to Kristina, beaming. "My granddaughter. My beautiful granddaughter." He stroked her face like it was the first time he'd seen her. . . . It *was* the first time. "You get to come with me for a little while."

"I do?"

"You do," he said, nodding. "It's time for you to learn some things in the Beyond. You just needed someone to show you how to get there."

Kristina shot me a look of panic, and I shot her the exact same one back, and before I knew it, he took her hand and held tight.

"She'll be back soon, Baylor," he said. "I promise."

And with that, both of them walked forward and disappeared. They were gone. It was just me standing alone in the empty kitchen, stunned.

That's when I started crying. I ran to my parents' room, and I sobbed to them about how Grandpa had taken Kristina to somewhere else and I couldn't see them anymore.

The kicker, of course, was that my dad didn't know his father had passed away yet. Both of them shot up in bed and looked at me, each distinctly terrified of the answer to their next question.

"Which grandpa was it, Baylor?"

"Grandpa Bosco," I whimpered, and I watched my dad fall apart in bed. I didn't get why he was so upset, and frankly, I was more upset that he was crying harder than I was and getting all the attention from my mom.

"He said to tell you he loves me and you and Mom and Jack," I said, trying to return the focus to my problem, but it only seemed to make him feel worse. "Then he grabbed Kristina, and they both left!"

"Honey, I'm sorry they're gone, but your father is *very* sad right now," my mom said with quiet exasperation, clutching my dad's head during his heaving.

"Mom, I'm sad too!" I cried. "What am I going to do without Kristina?"

That was a tough year for everyone. Just as my father mourned his father, I mourned the loss of my sister. Strangely enough, it was the first time I began to understand death.

The questions. The permanency. The heartache.

It took her 367 days to come back. I had never felt so lonely, and now that she was gone for the first time in years, a small but very distinct part of me began to panic.

Kristina had apparently learned a lot about her role in my life during our year apart. Whenever we mention that year, she always laughs because it didn't feel that long to her. To her it seemed like a long day of classes.

But she always emphasizes the *long* part. She's told me only bits and pieces—what she's allowed to tell me so far—but one thing she learned is that she was never meant to be alive. Kristina was always meant to be my companion in life, just as I was always meant to be able to communicate with dead people. We were slotted to be a two-person team from the very beginning, and maybe even before then. I was to be the message giver, and she was to be a sort of spirit manager—a buffer between the physical world and the Beyond.

Before she disappeared for that year, I could see ghosts, but I never communicated with them, nor could I block them out. Even during that year she was gone, the ghosts kept their distance, though I could still see and hear them. When she got back from the Beyond, she seemed different—older and more confident—and she told me it was time to start relaying messages to allow people to heal.

Then the floodgates opened. The ghosts that had always hovered nearby suddenly swarmed me, drowning me with their nonstop chatter, desperate pleas, and sometimes scary images.

Kristina helped me out immensely. Whenever I had a problem, she was there. She was the one who came up with my daily routine. Once I started lighting my candle every morning to surround myself with light and positivity, talking to spirits became a bit easier.

At first my mom refused to buy me a candle and my own lighter. I was much too young to be playing with fire, she'd say. But after my dad reminded her that I was also too young to deal with talking to dead people, she gave in.

But then she wouldn't let me keep the candle in my room, or let me light it. She didn't understand why it was so important. But who could expect her to? How was she supposed to know that, without that positive energy, I could see menacing phantoms with creepy, glowing green eyes circling the house? How was she supposed to know that the light kept away the negative spirits who had left unfinished business on Earth? Heck, how was I supposed to know that, without Kristina guiding me?

When I tried explaining it to my mom, she threw me into the car and drove to the community church, where she made the reverend bless me with some sort of spiritual protection prayer. It actually helped a little bit, but Kristina told me that any prayers from any person of any faith were always good.

Afterward Mom explained my gift to Reverend Henry, and he became the first person outside of my family to know what I could do. I think my mom had expected him to deny it, to refute her claim, but he didn't. Instead he knelt down beside me and whispered, "You have a very special gift, Baylor. Use it wisely. I'm always here if you need help."

After that my mom started asking me every day how Kristina was doing.

"Is she . . . is she happy?" she'd ask, usually while

fidgeting with my lunch box before school. I'd look over at Kristina, who would nod ferociously in her delight over our mom's change of heart.

"She's nodding yes," I'd say.

My mom would sigh, her shoulders sinking low. "Good, good. I'm glad to hear that."

But if my mom asked about her today, what would I say? That she had been ghostnapped? That she wasn't by my side for the first time in more than four years and I was trying not to panic?

Unlike with a missing breathing person, no one could help me find a missing ghost. It was just me, with absolutely no resources except to ask other random ghosts if they'd seen the girl version of me walking around.

Of course, they all said no.

My mind jumped to all sorts of conclusions, ranging from *She got lost on the way back from the Beyond and is in some undiscovered universe* to *The Sheet Man is holding her hostage, and it's up to me to track them down.*

The only consolation of that morning was that I was so distracted by the poking doctors and prodding nurses and pestering parents that forgetting to panic wasn't so hard. By the time I was discharged, when my dad had already left for work and my mom was waiting with Ella to take me home, I had a plan.

"We need to make a pit stop before home," I said gravely.

"We do?" my mom asked.

"Don't worry. You'll appreciate this particular stop."

Demon shoes are never in style.

FIFTEEN MINUTES LATER WE WERE AT THE community church. I needed some sort of higher-power blessing this morning, and if I didn't have Kristina or my candles, Reverend Henry was the next-best thing. Plus, it had been a while since he had done any protections on me, and I secretly hoped that the barrier between me and the spirits had become more malleable because his auxiliary protections had lapsed.

Leaving my mom in a pew with Ella, I found Reverend Henry back in his office, talking to someone on the phone.

He grinned when he saw me and held up his finger.

"Yes, I know that's how you're feeling right now, but you'll soon see that it's worth it. I promise you."

He made a funny face and tapped his thumb rapidly against his fingers, the universal sign for *Yada, yada, yada, this broad won't shut up.*

A couple of minutes later he hung up the phone and widened his eyes to ghost size.

"Women, I tell ya!" he said jokingly. "My daughter, calling from her dorm room and panicked that she picked the wrong college to attend."

"She's somewhere in Texas, right?"

"Yep. In Austin. She thinks it's too far away, she misses home and family and proper seasons, she thinks she should transfer, and so on and so forth. You know, normal teenager stuff." He leaned back in his seat. "But enough about my daughter. What brings you here, Baylor? Shouldn't you be in school right now?"

"Things aren't too great, Rev," I said, before launching into the events of the previous few days.

"And I just left the hospital and came directly here," I finished. "Help me."

"That is some story, Baylor," he said slowly. "Wow. Well, first things first, you didn't get to do your routine today, so let's light some candles."

Four candles and a hundred deep breaths later I felt the calmest I'd felt all morning.

"Now," he said, returning to his chair, "maybe you'll have some peace of mind to think. I'm sure Kristina will return soon too. I guess the good thing about her being dead already is that you don't have to involve police."

"Except that when she goes missing, there's no one to help me at all."

"True," he said, lifting his legs up and crossing his feet on his desk. "But as you said, she's probably in the Beyond learning some more ways to protect you. It's likely just taking a while, since you both have never faced anything like this before."

He kept talking, but I'd stopped paying attention because I'd noticed his shoes, and a deep chill ran down my back.

"Reverend," I said, interrupting him, my eyes fixated on his feet. "Where did you get those shoes?"

"These?" He laughed. "Believe it or not, they're actually from a big donation we got from some out-of-towners. I needed a new pair, and I saw they were sort of run-down, but they seemed like a nice brand, nothing I could ever afford, so I thought, *Hey, why not?* Owning some secondhand name-brand shoes for once won't kill me." He paused for a moment and seemed perplexed. "I think it won't kill me, at least. Why do you ask? Can you tell they're old?"

"No," I said. "They're the same shoes the Sheet Man was wearing."

His face fell. "Are you telling me I'm wearing demon shoes?"

"I don't know what I'm telling you," I said, leaning forward to examine the silver buckles. "I just know they look like the ones I saw before the tuba fell on me. When did they arrive?"

"Uh, last week at some point. Thursday, probably."

"Thursday was the first day the Sheet Man visited!" I nearly yelped with excitement. "Who made the donation?"

"I honestly couldn't tell you," he said, taking his legs off the desk and slipping the shoes off. "But now I think I'm going to burn them."

"That's not the worst idea, but let me see them first."

He set them on the edge of the desk. I hesitated for a moment because I was worried what I was going to see by touching the shoes. There was a big chance any memories attached to them were brutal.

But when I picked one up, nothing happened. I turned it all over in my hands, running my fingers along the seams on the side and tracing the edge of the buckle, as if trying to massage a memory out of it, but it was just a normal shoe. The leather was so soft that I felt bad for telling Reverend Henry that they were probably cursed—I could tell they were comfortable.

On the inside, just under the shoe's tongue, I saw something written in black marker. I squinted, but it was blurry, like it had been written a hundred years ago.

"There's something written there," I said, getting my phone out to shine some light on it. "Can you make it out? I think the first letter is an *A*."

The reverend took the shoe and peered inside. "Sort of looks like it says 'APARKER.'" He tilted his hand and moved the shoe an inch away from his face. "I think it says that, at least."

"What's an aparker?" He handed back the shoe and I looked again. It did sort of look like that.

"It's probably a name, like A. Parker, with the *A* being an initial."

"What kind of man writes his name on his shoes? Especially a pair this nice."

"I can't say. Could be any reason."

"I wonder if I could track him down online. At least I have something to work with." I held out the shoe, smiling. "You can have this back now."

He threw his hands up. "I don't want to touch that thing again."

"Oh, come on," I said. "You've been wearing them for a few days now. I think they're fine. I didn't feel anything negative when I touched them."

He still looked hesitant. "I'll wear them for today because I'll be barefoot otherwise," he said. "But tonight they're going straight into the fire."

I told my mom the news in the car, but she didn't share in my excitement.

"You didn't tell me you saw that thing wearing shoes! And the reverend was wearing the same shoes?!" She gasped. "Oh my God, I hope you incinerated them on the spot!"

"I don't think they're cursed," I said. "They didn't have a bad energy."

"Well, it can't be a good energy, Baylor!" she said.

"They're just shoes," I said. "They're fine."

"Well, you're a boy, so you don't get it, but if I found out my shoes belonged to a dead lady who was haunting me, I wouldn't be very happy. I'd probably even demand a refund."

Mom agreed to let me take the rest of the day off instead of going back to school. At home there was a gigantic package of baked goods sitting on the kitchen table, courtesy of Aiden's mom. She really *had* baked a lot: There were cookies, brownies, blondies, seven-layer bars, and a small lemon cake. I grabbed a cookie, ran upstairs, lit a candle, and hopped onto my computer. Just as I was about to start searching the web for some more clues about the Sheet Man, my computer started to fritz. The screen blurred for a few seconds, then turned blue.

Then, letter by letter, a message appeared on the screen.

Don't worry about me. Be back soon. K.

Then it disappeared.

"Well, that's just great," I mumbled to myself. At least she wasn't in danger. Still, she could have given me some idea of when she'd return. I told my grandma that I'd see her soon all the time, even though I had no idea when the next time would be. It could be a year, for all I knew.

"Soon" was what you said to comfort someone. I didn't want to be comforted. I wanted my sister back to help me solve this problem.

Think logically. You're being followed by something Kristina thinks is really bad. She wouldn't leave you for a long time, since she knows you need her help. She will be back soon, and by "soon" she means shortly.

Feeling a bit better after rationalizing away my paranoia, I took to the Internet to dig up information on A. Parker.

First I typed in "A. Parker shoes." Nothing.

Next I tried "A. Parker sheets." Still nothing.

Then I typed in "A. Parker, Keene, New Hampshire."

It turned up some results, but nothing too specific. I tried to think of what else I knew that would be helpful, and then I smacked my hand to my forehead.

"Of course!" I added one word to the search bar: "obituary."

Jackpot. It turned out an Alfred Parker had died some three years earlier in Winchester, a nearby town. He'd been seventy-two when he died, been divorced, and had a son and a daughter. Seemed he was a late starter with having kids—both of them were only in their midtwenties when he died. It looked like he'd remarried, too. It didn't state what he'd done for work, just that he'd "pursued many successful entrepreneurial endeavors."

He seemed relatively normal. Nothing screamed that he would transform into a creepy demon stalker.

I read it once more and stopped at the line about the children, Isabella and William.

I had a feeling they would be my best bet, so I searched for them next. The results were limited, though, with just a few viable entries before everything devolved into sign-ups for online yellow pages. But I did find some pertinent information, like some old articles about Alfred and their mom, Rosalie T. Parker, and even some old photos. I managed to figure out Isabella was in California working as a teacher, and William was going to school in Boston.

William seemed the most promising, since Boston was only a couple of hours away from Keene.

The only problem was figuring out how to get there.

"Absolutely not," my mom said when I told her about my discoveries. She was sitting on the floor of the family room playing with Ella, and I was shoving down a brownie. "I am not driving you to Boston so you can attempt to meet up with the son of the dead guy who put you in the hospital. End of discussion."

"But, Mom," I said, my mouth filled with chocolate, "what if he needs my help?"

"Baylor, haven't you mentioned several times now that Kristina can't confront him because he's evil? Maybe he should have thought about getting help before he died and had to face the consequences of his poor life decisions." She looked at Ella and cooed, "Isn't that right, Ella-Bella? You make good choices in life! Good choices!"

"Good!" Ella screamed, throwing a block into the air.

"That's right!" My mom laughed. "Good girl. Don't be bad, or else your brother will have to deal with you from the Beyond, and we don't want that."

"So that's it?" I asked, annoyed. "What if I ask Dad?"

"Don't bother. Even if he were up for it, I am forbidding you to go."

"Forbidding? Mom, I can talk to dead people because I'm supposed to pass along healing messages. You're preventing me from doing my life's duty. You realize that, right?"

"I've grown to appreciate your gift and think it's wonderful that you can help people who need it," she said as she scooped up Ella and headed to the kitchen. "But when you wind up in the hospital because of it, guess what? I get to put my foot down. And if someone on the other side has a problem with it, you tell them I would be *more* than happy to discuss that with them." She kissed me on the cheek. "Got it?"

11

Consider developing your whittling skills.

THE NEXT DAY AT SCHOOL EVERY TIME MY classmates saw me, they would stare awkwardly or say something like, "Feeling okay, Baylor?" Apparently, news had traveled to everyone about my collision with a tuba.

To make matters worse, Kristina still hadn't reappeared. I lit five candles that morning and asked her to come back, but when I got done with my shower and looked in the mirror, there was a message written in the fog.

Stop being a baby,

It freaked me out she had been there without even saying hi. I just hoped she couldn't see me in the shower. The mere thought made me shudder.

At lunchtime I told Aiden that it seemed like everyone was making a bigger deal out of the incident than they should be.

"Well," he said, unpacking his usual pepperoni sandwich, "they're not talking about your accident as much as they are the fact that you screamed like a banshee and had the scariest face any of us have ever seen outside of a movie."

"What?"

"Yeah, people think you're haunted or something," he said, shrugging. "Not everyone gets what you can do."

"That sucks!" I said, slamming the table. "Being in band is bad enough for my reputation. I don't need that rumor on top of it."

"You should know that what people think of you doesn't matter," he said pointedly.

He was right. How many times had I passed on messages from ghosts saying they wished they had lived their lives the way they wanted instead of the way others wanted? Too many to count.

But still . . . junior high is hard enough without ghosts yammering in your ear, and I needed all the help I could get.

"How's that head, Baylor?" J asked, stopping at our table on the way to her next class. She wasn't in our lunch period, thankfully; otherwise, Aiden would be in danger of choking to death every day.

"A bit sore," I said. "Too bad people think I'm haunted."

She smiled. "Well, better to be haunted than stupid." Aiden was grinning like an idiot at his sandwich the whole time. "Uh, are *you* okay, Aiden?"

"Yeah, yeah, fine, fine," he said, looking up at her. "Just pretty happy about this pepperoni, is all."

I turned my head and closed my eyes. It was so painful to watch *and* hear.

"Well, enjoy," she said, shaking her head. "Let's hang out this week? Maybe head to the Patty Joint on Friday night?"

"Sounds good," I said as she walked away.

I let a moment pass before turning to him. "Seriously? You're going to die alone."

"I know," he said, taking a bite of his sandwich. "I know."

After school I had an injury-free band practice, although my ego was still slightly tarnished. Mr. G., in an effort to be nice, had placed pillows around my chair in case I collapsed again. My cheeks were on fire as I thanked him, but all he'd really done was inadvertently remind everyone that I was the crazy guy who'd had to go to the hospital.

But all the embarrassment melted away when I walked through the door of my bedroom and saw Kristina waiting for me on my bed.

She wasn't alone, though.

Standing beside her and gazing politely around my room was the ghost of a man dressed to the nines as an eighteenth-century British soldier, complete with leather kneecaps, a tricorn hat, and a vivid red coat.

"Is it . . . is it Halloween again?" I asked, looking the man up and down while he studied the picture of a Florida sunset that was hanging on my wall.

"There you are," Kristina said, rising. "Baylor, I'd like you to meet one of our spirit guides, Colonel Fleetwood."

The man turned and bowed slightly to me. "How do you do, Baylor?"

"I'm very well, thanks," I said. "How do you guys do?"

"Ugh, stop being awkward, Baylor," Kristina said. "Colonel Fleetwood is here to help us with the Sheet Man."

"Oh, good. Are you going to be able to capture him and compel his exit?" I asked.

"In a way, yes," he said. He had a pleasant face,

although his cryptic grin confused me: I couldn't tell if he was annoyed or amused to be here. Even odder was that he seemed way too young to be a soldier. I'd guess he was sixteen when he crossed over.

"So," I said, "how?"

"I hope you've kept up with your whittling skills," he said as Kristina smiled mischievously next to him.

A few hours later, in the dark of the night, I found myself wandering through the woods near my house and wondering what it would be like to be normal, to not have to talk to ghosts and construct talismans to ward off evil spirits.

"Tonight is the full moon," Kristina had said earlier, "so it's the perfect time to build it."

"You know I have homework, right? I need to write an English essay and try to understand the math lesson I missed yesterday. I don't have time for this."

"It must be done tonight, young lad!" Colonel Fleetwood said. "No other night will offer the protection that a full moon can."

"First off, 'young lad'? You're, like, two years older than me. Secondly, why can't I do it during the day, when the big ball of fire called the sun is shining? Doesn't that offer some protection?"

"The sun knows only light," the colonel said. "The moon, however, sees through the dark."

"Uh, okay," I said. "Did you get that from a fortune cookie?"

"A fortune cookie? I don't know what that is, but it sounds delightful!"

Kristina scoffed. "Stop, Baylor. The full moon offers the best protection because it illuminates even the darkest of nights. Isn't that obvious?"

It did make sense to me, in a way, but I couldn't figure out why they hadn't just brought over some high-powered ghost zapper from the Beyond to blow the Sheet Man up. Surely, *someone* over there had to be capable of stopping him.

Alas, they wouldn't hear of it. This situation was one I had to deal with head-on.

"I learned a bit more while I was gone," Kristina said, "and I think you were right, Baylor. Even though there's something seriously wrong here, I don't think the Sheet Man is purely evil."

"You learned a bit more? Who teaches you these things? Were you and the colonel sitting in a classroom taking notes from Buddha or something?"

"Shut up, Baylor. There's something bizarre going on, and we need to figure out how to help."

"And this talisman is going to stop him?" I asked.

"Oh, yes," Colonel Fleetwood said. "It's quite effective."

Before heading into the woods, I had been sort of excited, like we were going on a mystical adventure, just me, my ghost twin, and our British soldier spirit guide. But when they finally told me what I was looking for, my spirits fell, pun absolutely intended.

"I'm looking for a big piece of wood and a stone," I said. "You can't be serious." I had been expecting them to say we needed something really weird, like thirteen roses and the blood of a newborn deer.

But no. I needed some wood and a stone—the tools a caveman would use to crush bugs into paste. Not what I viewed as the ideal tools to keep a spirit from stalking me.

We trekked through the woods for a while, and an eerie silence seemed to permeate the air. My flashlight, in addition to the full moon, provided ample light, and yet there were no trees rustling, no birds chirping, no squirrels running amok, and heck, not even an earthworm wriggling around. I suspected the two energies walking alongside me had something to do with it.

I shone my flashlight on more than a hundred pieces of wood before finally finding one that Colonel Fleetwood deemed suitable. It was a part of a fallen branch, the snapped end just wide enough that I could hollow it out to fit a stone inside.

Then we went to a babbling brook nearby and searched for some stones. This hunt proved to be easier in terms of finding the perfect stone, since the only requirement was that it be as spherical as possible, yet getting it was infinitely more challenging because the water was probably forty degrees. It had to come from the water, though, because of some dumb rule about purity. All I know is that by the time we had found the perfect one, I could no longer feel my hand.

"Welcome to our world," Kristina said as the colonel nodded. "We don't feel a thing."

I rolled my eyes. Of course I wouldn't get any sympathy from the dead people.

Back home I found the jack-o'-lantern carving knives, which hadn't seen the inside of a pumpkin in a long time, and headed up to my room. Under the guidance of the colonel I sawed off the long, scraggly end of the branch, leaving me with a hunk of wood that resembled a thick hockey puck. Then I began whittling away at the wood bit by bit to create a deep enough space. I slowly carved for hours while I listened to the ghosts chat casually like they were old friends. Well, they probably were old friends, but it was still weird to hear Kristina chatting with someone who wasn't me.

"It felt quite strange, greeting my mother once she crossed over," the colonel said to Kristina as he leaned against the wall. "So I can only imagine how utterly unreal it will feel to you when you must do the same for yours."

"Your mom at least knew what you looked like," Kristina said. "Mine doesn't even know what color my hair is."

"She does too," I said. "I've told her a million times."

"Yeah, but she doesn't really know," Kristina said. "You didn't do that good of a job describing it."

"I repeated to her exactly what you told me to say!"

"Yeah, and it still wasn't very good."

"That side seems ready, lad," Colonel Fleetwood said, looking over my shoulder. "One more side to go and you'll have a good space there."

I nodded. "Got it."

He turned back to Kristina and said, "Did you hear from Lincoln what Selene said about the moon tonight? She was apparently in a bad mood and wanted to cover the sky with clouds, but he put a stop to that for us."

"As he should have," she said. "Everyone's too riled up for her to go doing something like that."

"Hopefully, it'll all be sorted out soon. This talisman should do the trick, and then I'll be able to be on my way."

"You're staying?" I asked, whipping my head around.

"Of course he is," Kristina said. "I told you I was bringing reinforcements."

"Oh. I didn't realize you meant *him*." I jerked my head toward the colonel. "I thought you meant someone like, I don't know, Jesus or Vishnu or someone like that."

Kristina and Fleetwood looked at each other for a loaded second before throwing their heads back in laughter.

"What! Why is that so funny?"

"I can't . . . I can't . . . s-speak!" Kristina sputtered.

After a few minutes she finally regained her composure, while I sat there, jaw clenched, whittling away like Mister Geppetto.

"Sorry, Baylor, I don't mean to laugh so hard," she said. "It's just that, well, this issue isn't really *that* serious. To put it in a way you might understand, it would be like dropping a nuclear bomb to kill a spider, rather than just using a rolled-up newspaper."

"He kills spiders?" the colonel asked, suddenly perturbed.

"I tell him not to," Kristina said, her voice going high. "He doesn't listen."

"Lad, you shouldn't do that!" he said. "Bad karma."

"Weren't you a soldier, Fleetwood?" I asked, totally aware of how annoyed I sounded. "Didn't you kill people when you were alive? How is killing a spider worse than that?"

"I was duty-bound to serve in a war," he said, nodding. "It was something I had no control over and believed to be justified."

"Well, I feel justified in killing spiders when they sneak up on me out of nowhere," I said. "They have double the legs of most animals. It's creepy. Why do they need that many legs? They're clearly monstrous animals, and I treat them as such."

He raised his eyebrows at Kristina, who slowly shook her head, but I didn't care because I felt like I had won the argument.

After I was done whittling, they instructed me to crack an egg downstairs and bring the shell back to my room.

"This is the stupidest thing I've ever done," I mumbled to myself, walking from the kitchen, eggshell in hand, and thinking of Fleetwood and his dumb accent. Why was Kristina even bothering to hang around him? There had to be better spirit guides in the Beyond besides that clown.

"Here we go," I said, presenting the shell to them. "One eggshell, at your service."

"Wonderful," Fleetwood said. "We're nearly there!"

"All you have to do now," Kristina said, "is put the stone inside the eggshell, close the shell up, and then place it in the center of the wooden bowl."

I furrowed my eyebrows. "Okay," I said slowly as I did as they instructed.

"And here we are," Fleetwood whispered, admiring the talisman. "Excellent work, Baylor. Now, if you'll kindly turn off your lights and light a candle for us."

I nodded, grabbing a fresh one from my nightstand and switching off the light before walking back. Illuminated by the glow of my computer's screen saver, I struck a match and lit the wick, which crackled violently.

"We're ready," the colonel said. He and Kristina positioned themselves around me, forming a small circle. "Baylor, place the talisman on the ground and keep hold of your candle. Good. Now, what I need you to do is very simple: Imagine the light of your candle enveloping the talisman with positive energy, and all the while think the words, 'With this tool I will only do good.'"

I shut my eyes and imagined the flame spreading out from its home on the wick and encircling the talisman.

With this tool I will only do good.
With this tool I will only do good.
With this tool I will only do good.

I opened my eyes and nearly dropped the candle. A thin golden ribbon was slowly slicing through the air, like a river on fire, heading right for the talisman, where it began to shoot around the way an asteroid would orbit Earth, quickly, blindingly, securing the wooden bowl into its web of flames.

I watched with awe, longing to touch it just to see what would happen.

"Uh, Kristina? You never told me I could do this."

"Not now, Baylor," Kristina murmured. She extended her hands, palms down, over the talisman and calmly said, "Spread your light." And from her hands emerged that same blue light that she had used to send away the meddlesome spirit at the hospital. It pulsed out of her in feeble waves, eventually joining the candlelight and turning the sphere electric blue.

Colonel Fleetwood mimicked Kristina's hand position and said, "Find your purpose." The waves of light

that emitted from his hands were shockingly white, hitting the blue and gold with a sharp hiss and causing
the whole thing to swell and burn white, like a small
supernova.

After several seconds of staring at the inferno,
both amazed by what was happening and worried that
my retinas were burning, a fierce, powerful sensation
boomed from within me, like I was made of fire, and
I found myself saying, "Love conquers all," in unison
with Kristina and the colonel, both of whom seemed
completely unsurprised.

And then, as soon as the last word escaped our
mouths, the ribbons of energy dissipated, the lights in
my room turned themselves back on, and the wooden
bowl on the ground was . . . still a wooden bowl.

I bent down to pick it up and noticed it looked
exactly the same, except for one small change.

"The shell isn't broken anymore," I gasped, as if
that were really the most amazing thing that had
happened in the last two minutes. I jerked the bowl
around and noticed the egg wasn't rolling around
either, like it was glued to the wood.

"The stone is sealed inside," Colonel Fleetwood
said. "The next time you are visited by the Sheet
Man, crack the egg open and throw the stone at him.
You'll find your troubles will end there."

12

NEVER eat at
Italian restaurants.

I HAD TO CARRY THE TALISMAN WITH ME everywhere, just in case the Sheet Man appeared at a random time. That meant putting this strange wooden bowl into my backpack at school and trying to hide it from my classmates. The last thing I wanted was for people to know that the haunted band geek carried around a goofy-looking wooden bowl with an egg in it.

At school the next day, I had the pleasure of having both Kristina and Fleetwood following me around. My very own ghost entourage. Kristina was

having the time of her life. She usually had to sit
in silence and learn all the things she already knew,
but today she and Fleetwood were basically having a
party. They were going on and on in my English class
about something hysterical Shakespeare had said to
Hemingway, until finally I glared at Kristina, and she
and the colonel went to wait outside.

"Sorry, Baylor," she said as I walked out after the
bell rang. "I forgot that you actually have to concentrate in class."

"It's fine," I said. "It's not like the ending of *Julius
Caesar* is a big surprise."

"It was to him," Fleetwood said gravely. "He's still a
touch bitter about it, even after all these years."

After band practice I found my mom waiting for me
outside. I was surprised to see her, since I'd planned
for Aiden's mom to give me a ride home.

"What are you doing here?" I asked. "Hey, Jack.
Hi, Ella." Ella smiled at me with sheer delight while
Jack waved feebly.

"It's your great-aunt's birthday, remember?" my
mom said. "You forgot, didn't you?"

"I was in the hospital three days ago for a possible concussion, remember?" I said. "You forgot,
didn't you?"

"Don't be smart with me, Baylor Bosco," she said. "I've told you since the beginning of October about this dinner."

"How old is she, anyway?"

"The woman's turning eighty-eight!"

"Why are we having this dinner? That's such a random number. If she were ninety, I'd understand."

"Baylor, when you get to be eighty-eight years old, every year that you don't die is an accomplishment. I know that concept may be difficult for someone like you to grasp, but for the rest of us it's a big deal."

"I guess I get it," I said. "Where are we going?"

"Carrino's!" Jack said from the backseat.

I glanced at Jack, then turned my head slowly to my mom; she had her lips pursed, and her eyes were focused squarely in front of her, pretending like she didn't notice my glare.

"You have got to be kidding me," I hissed. "If you had mentioned the name of the restaurant, I wouldn't have forgotten about the dinner. You are a sneaky, sneaky woman."

"I'm sorry, Baylor, but it's her favorite restaurant, and it's *her* birthday. She's eighty-eight! What can I do?"

I shook my head, furious about the way this night was unfolding.

"Is there a problem with this establishment?" the colonel asked Kristina in the back.

"Baylor can't tune spirits out in Italian restaurants," she said. "We don't know why. He thinks it's the garlic. I think it's because Italians are known for their personable energy. Whatever the reason, whenever we go to an Italian place, it's usually a disaster."

"Dis-aws-ta," Ella squeaked, banging her doll on the window.

"Oh, how precious!" Fleetwood said, waving at Ella. "The child understands us."

"Come to think of it," Kristina said slowly, "Ella's never been to an Italian restaurant. I wonder how she's going to react."

My great-aunt Hilda had been married a long time ago, sometime in her thirties, but had never had children. Her husband had been a rich man, but no one seemed to talk about him much. I always got the impression he'd had ties to the mob, a suspicion that his early, mysterious demise seemed to confirm.

She had lived alone for the better of forty years, and since she had no other family, she nearly always joined our holiday celebrations, as well as any meaningful milestones, unfortunately for me.

The problem was that, despite being an agreeable

lady in most other facets of her life, Aunt Hilda was a firm nonbeliever in my gift. It's not just that she didn't believe I could communicate with the dead, but that she was very vocal to anyone who would listen that her grandnephew was a charlatan who played on people's emotions and gave them a false sense of hope about whatever comes after death.

It didn't bother me that she didn't believe me, but it did bother me that she openly called me a liar in front of strangers and family alike. We eventually learned never to bring up my gift in front of her, and if she even hinted around to it, we would change the subject faster than you could blink.

When we arrived at Carrino's that night, I was not in a good mood. I had Colonel British McBad-Teeth clinging to my twin, I knew I wasn't going to be able to tune out any of the spirits inside, and I would have to act like none of it was bothering me, all because my crazy great-aunt had decided to live another year.

Carrino's had big glass doors for the entryway, and from the outside I couldn't see or hear any spirits. It was one of the best Italian spots in town, though, so I knew it was going to be busy even on a random Thursday night. I walked up to the doors, took one final breath, and shot one last nasty glance at my mom, who was following me with Ella in her arms and a worried frown on her face.

With my eyes closed, I opened the doors and was immediately overcome by the noise. It was a small restaurant, and everything was amplified by the picture-frame-covered walls.

When I opened my eyes, I couldn't even see the tables anymore. It was like leaving the stadium after a Patriots game and getting caught in the middle of a million people taking half steps toward the exit, hoping not to get trampled by the crowd.

The difference was that I could tune out the ghosts at stadiums. At the restaurant it was so packed I couldn't tell who was dead or alive. I motioned for my mom to pass me so I could follow her lead. Otherwise, I'd be running into people I thought were dead, and I'd be awkwardly scooting around and saying "Excuse me" to people I could walk right through.

But she wouldn't go, because as soon as she walked by me with Ella, the baby began to scream one of those deep-from-the-gut, almost primal screams. The kind where you know something is really wrong.

"Ella!" my mom said. "What's wrong, Ella-Bella? You were fine just a second ago."

"It's packed, Mom," I said. "It's packed, and it's loud."

My mom tilted her head and frowned, walking back outside as a high-pitched voice chirped from behind me.

"Um, we're actually not packed at all," the tiny hostess said from her stand as a man with a thick black mustache leaned over and tried to smell her. She didn't mind, though, since he was dead. "We have plenty of available tables for your party if you'd like to sit."

"I, uh, that's not actually what I meant," I said, fumbling for words, trying to catch the spirit's eye over her shoulder so he'd know I could see him. "We actually have reservations for a birthday dinner."

"Oh, are you with Renee O'Brien's party?"

"Yeah, that's my grandma," I said, still focusing on the area just to the left of the hostess, where the man was now rubbing the girl's shoulder with his hands. She frowned at me, but then I saw her shiver. She could sense the man's presence but had no idea what was going on.

Luckily, Kristina turned her attention away from the colonel to realize what was happening, and she zapped him with her blue energy.

"It was just getting good!" he wailed as he faded into nothing.

"Ugh!" Kristina groaned.

"Follow me," said the hostess, and once she turned her back, I grimaced at Kristina, who, along with the colonel, smiled encouragingly.

"I daresay you've got this under control, lad," the colonel said. "At least you're not charging onto a battlefield on a cold, wintry morning, knowing that it will soon be smeared with your blood, and the blood of all the fine gentlemen you're leading."

"You are not helping right now, Fleetwood," I muttered as we passed a group of people I could only assume were alive. They turned and stared, and I raised my eyebrows at them awkwardly, not wanting to respond in case they were really dead. It would only make the people sitting at the next table feel uncomfortable.

"You're right here," the hostess said, sitting us down at the eight-seat table. We were the first ones to arrive, thankfully, so I took my seat at the end, and Jack sat right across from me. It was the sort of restaurant that put white paper on top of the tables to serve as both a tablecloth and a canvas for kids to draw on. The hostess set down crayons, and Jack went right to work.

As he was writing his name in awkward cursive letters, he leaned forward and whispered, "See anyone?"

"Yeah," I whispered back. "Lots."

He drew a sharp breath. "This isn't going to be very fun."

"Nope."

My mom got to the table a few minutes later. She'd managed to calm Ella down, but the girl was fidgeting, and it was obvious that she was like a leaky gas pipe just one spark away from an explosion.

"There are my sweet grandchildren!" Grandma said, barreling through a group of ghosts.

"Grandma!" Jack said, throwing down his crayon and jumping up to hug her.

"Hi, Wacky Jacky," she said. "Did you have a good day at school?"

"Yeah, I played four square today and only lost twice."

"I'm so impressed!" She turned to me and hesitated for a moment, knowing exactly what I was thinking. "Sorry, Baylor, but she insisted."

I got up and hugged her. "It's all right. It's just for a couple of hours. Honestly, Ella's the one you're going to have to worry about. She can see them everywhere."

She looked at Ella, and her jaw dropped upon seeing her granddaughter squirming in her seat, her head twisting around every few seconds as she looked at all the passing spirits.

"Oh my . . . ," she said. "Maybe I should have tried a little harder to make my dear sister change her mind."

Speak of the devil, Aunt Hilda crossed through the group of ghosts she would never believe I could see, gently led by Grandpa By (his longtime nickname since being cruelly christened Byron O'Brien).

I was the first one she saw, and if she was already annoyed with me, it wasn't apparent.

"Baylor, come help your ancient auntie get into her chair, will ya?" she said.

I grabbed on to her other arm and pulled the chair out for her. She plopped into it, reaching up to grab my neck and pull me down for a kiss. "It's good to see ya, kid. Can you believe this broad is eighty-eight?"

"You don't look a day over one hundred, Aunt Hilda," I said.

She threw her head back, clutching the half-heart necklace she always wore, the laughter croaking out of her mouth like an ad campaign against smoking, and said, "You slay me. Jacky boy, come here and give me a kiss."

As Jack clambered up from his seat again, Grandpa By pulled me aside and said, "You doing okay?"

I nodded. "They're everywhere. And they're loud. Ella sees them too."

"I told Renee not to come here. I said to her, '*Renee,* you remember what happened last time we went to an Italian joint?' And she says to me—get this— she says, 'Yeah, By, but Hilda's eighty-eight years old, how many more chances is she gonna have to eat some Italian food?'" He threw his hands up. "If tonight goes poorly, let me tell you, it's gonna be her last time, I'll say that much. I'll say that much." He crossed his arms over his chest. "And you with the hospital visit this week, and the weird appearances from things I don't like to imagine too much, and the bad Halloween experience. How could it not go poorly?"

I shook my head. "You're reading my mind, Grandpa."

"Don't say that, kid," he said. "With you it could come true. I'll tell you, it's going to be a fiasco. But the lady is eighty-eight, and we're here, so we will deal with it, grandson, we will *deal* with it as all O'Brien men do. I know your last name is that Bosco nonsense, but I like to pretend it's O'Brien sometimes, you know?"

My dad arrived shortly after, and dinner finally got under way.

Right from the start everything went wrong. A ghost pretending to be the waiter came right up to

me, introduced himself as Charlie, and asked what
I'd like to drink.

"Uh, do you have hot chocolate?" I said, looking
up at him and not realizing anything was wrong. "I'm
sort of cold."

"Oh my word, he's already starting it," Aunt Hilda
groaned. I looked at her and then looked back at the
ghost, who was now lit up with blue and fading away.
Kristina had zapped him, but the damage was already
done.

"Oh, ha, ha, I was just, uh, practicing my Italian
for when the waiter comes, Aunt Hilda," I said. "You
didn't give me a chance to finish."

Everyone at the table was staring at me expectantly.

"Make something up," Kristina whispered. "Just
say some gibberish, she'll never know."

"*Fl-flomargo deechay en la . . . en la dulce,*" I said, doing
my best Mario and Luigi impression. My mom put
her hand up to her forehead and shut her eyes, while
my dad laughed silently behind his napkin. *"Encardo la
noche de dudo! Bravo!"*

A brutal moment of silence passed, until finally
Grandpa spoke up.

"Well, that was just amazing," he said sincerely. "I
didn't know you've been learning Italian."

"Yeah," I said, looking down, my cheeks probably

the color of the tomato sauce I'd be eating soon. "Getting pretty good at it."

"I bet," he said, his lips threatening to smile.

I shook my head and glared at Kristina, who said, "Sorry! I wasn't paying attention."

After that she and Colonel Fleetwood stood guard around my seat, making sure no other spirits could goof with me.

I stayed mostly silent for dinner, only giving short answers whenever someone asked me a question. I stole a blue crayon from Jack and kept drawing the shape of a candle flame, over and over again, until I realized I had created what sort of looked like a massive thunderstorm, the blue flames doubling as raindrops. I chuckled to myself as my food came out, and for that moment I felt pretty good about my spaghetti and meatballs.

Then I just had to ruin everything by going for the cheese.

I picked up the little jar of Parmesan cheese sitting in the middle of the table, unaware as usual that there was a memory attached to it. I was sucked into a vision of a man arguing with his wife at our same table. The vision was just a split second, but once it ended, I gasped and dropped the jar of cheese, causing it to plume all over my shirt and the table.

"I'm sorry," I said, still breathing heavily, "I'm sorry, I'm so clumsy."

Grandma noticed right away that something was wrong. I'd bet money that my face was as white as the ruined Parmesan.

"Baylor, why don't you get cleaned up in the bathroom," she said helpfully.

Except the second I stood up, I realized it wasn't helpful at all. Navigating through a minefield would have been easier than navigating through all the people in the restaurant. I shot a look at Kristina, and she nodded, leading the way for me.

Kristina made sure the ghosts didn't disturb me while I was sitting with our family, but as far as they were concerned, I was fair game while walking to the bathroom.

"Finally, you're up!" a twentysomething shouted at me excitedly. "I need you to tell my mom that I didn't kill myself! It was an accident, through and through. Look at me, I'm too good-looking to have wanted to die that young."

I glared at him, and he smirked. "What, are you a mute now? I know you can speak English, and some really bad fake Italian, too. Go tell her, she's right there." He pointed to his right at a woman with short black hair.

I shook my head and tried to communicate with my eyes, but it didn't work.

"You can't leave me here," he said, his voice faltering. "I'm not comfortable going to the Beyond until I know that she knows that."

Kristina and I exchanged glances. I was given this gift for this exact reason, but at the same time I was only five feet from my table, and if Aunt Hilda overheard me, she was going to say that I ruined her birthday by parading around the restaurant and that I couldn't even give her one special night.

Kristina bit her lip, clearly thinking the exact same thing.

Finally Colonel Fleetwood stepped in. "Perhaps you could use your energy to direct your mother toward the back of the establishment, so they could engage in a conversation in private?"

The ghost looked at him, then back at me.

"Are you kidding me with this guy?" he asked. "Really?"

I didn't respond, but he shrugged. "Whatever." And then he turned to his mom, bent over, and whispered in her ear. Midconversation, as her friends watched in confusion, the woman got up from the table and nearly ran to the bathrooms at the back of the restaurant, down a narrow hallway. I followed her path, listening to her son describe the sordid details of his death while sidestepping all the dead people, and cornered her before she went inside.

"Ma'am!" I hissed. "Ma'am, stop!"

She turned around. "Are you talking to me?"

"My name is Baylor Bosco, and I can communicate with people who have crossed over," I said. "Listen, Terri, what I'm going to say won't be easy to hear, but you need to hear it. Chad didn't kill himself. He needs you to know that it was an accident, that he would never have taken all those pills if he'd known it was going to kill him."

She recoiled in shock, then looked around the hallway and clutched the walls. Her mouth was moving, but no sound came out. Her hands shot to her chest and she stared at me in panic.

"Oh man, this is bad," Chad said.

"What's wrong with her?" I asked.

"She's having an asthma attack," he said. "You need to go get her inhaler from her purse."

My eyes bulged out. "What? No! I can't just go rummage through her purse!"

"Just say you found her back here like this and you saw where she got up from!" Kristina said.

"Oh my God," I said, turning around and sprinting to her table the same way I'd just come. An old woman was walking toward the bathroom, and I ran right for her, thinking I'd pass through her just fine.

It was like a rhino colliding with a bowling pin. The whole restaurant went silent as we tumbled to the floor, our limbs flying in every direction.

"Dear Lord!" my dad yelled, running over to help us as a few others from random tables did the same.

"I'm sorry, I'm sorry!" I said, overwhelmed by all the people around me, confused that no one was speaking and that the only thing I could hear was a loud man singing about pizza pies and *amore*. "There's a woman by the bathroom! She collapsed and needs her inhaler!"

A man turned, peeked around the corner to see the other woman on the floor, and yelled at the top of his lungs, "He's right! That woman needs an inhaler!"

As my dad pulled me up from the ground to brush me off and examine the cut on my elbow, another man ran toward the bathroom, presumably with the inhaler in his hands.

I honestly didn't think things could get worse, until they did.

The woman I had stampeded over wasn't responding, so they had to call 911. Then a couple of patrons got into an argument about whether I ran into her on purpose, with one of them swearing I had been looking right at her and had known exactly what I was doing, and the other saying that I had panicked trying to help the woman who was having an asthma attack and simply hadn't seen her.

Once Terri recovered from her asthma attack, she started spouting off that I had caused her attack by telling her I could talk to dead people and that I'd told her that her son didn't commit suicide. She wasn't saying it in an accusatory way, though. Rather, she was thrilled, saying she had heard of me before and wondered if she'd ever get the chance to meet me.

This revelation caused nearly all the ghosts and patrons in the restaurant to talk at once, and all I could do was stare as the people and sounds blurred together into one, while a couple of paramedics worked on the still-unconscious lady on the ground.

Moments away from passing out, I looked at Kristina, who pointed to the table next to her and said, "Spread the light." I looked at the candle for a second, forgetting what it could do for me, and then I stumbled over, picked it up, and imagined the white light surrounding me. Suddenly my mind cleared.

Feeling rejuvenated, I stood on a chair and shouted, "Everyone, shut up!"

For the next ten minutes I acted as the conductor of a symphony of healing messages, one after the other, pointing at person after person and delivering messages rapid-fire.

"You," I said, pointing at a woman in a purple dress, "your husband says buy the green house, not the blue one."

"But I like the blue one more!"

"You," I said, pointing at the man with extra-large ears, "your brother says thank you for taking care of his children after he died."

He nodded, a strong blush blazing across his face.

"You," I said to the man with too much hair gel, "your mother says lay off the hair gel."

"But it's in style!"

"You," I said to the teenage girl who had been weeping for the last few minutes, "your father says you won't believe this is really him, and that the only way you'll believe it is if he brings up the giraffe tattoo you got on your back in memory of him, and he wants you to know that he hates it, and that if you get another one, he's not going to be able to rest in peace."

And so on and so forth until everyone in the restaurant was stunned into silence.

Everyone except for one person.

"He's a *fraud*," Aunt Hilda croaked from her seat, refusing to look at me and studying her necklace with great interest. "He's nothing more than a parasite feeding off your sadness. He made it all up, you fools."

Everyone looked at her for a few seconds, no one saying a word. Then the weeping girl walked over, lifted up the back of her shirt to reveal a tattoo of a giraffe with the word "Dad" scrawled between the spots, and silently walked away.

13

Even ghosts can lose their tempers.

THE AFTERMATH OF THE DINNER WASN'T pretty. Even though nearly everyone in the restaurant was satisfied with their messages, and the woman whom I'd plowed to the ground woke up and got a message from her husband, and a journalist showed up to write an article about the event, my mom was still mortified.

"You turned her birthday into a sideshow for your gift, Baylor," my mom ranted on the drive home. "Aunt Hilda will always look back on her eighty-eighth birthday and remember your . . . your . . . *shenanigans.*"

"Shenanigans?" I said incredulously. "It's not like I stood on the table naked and danced, Mom. You're the one who forced me to go to that Italian restaurant, so if you didn't want that to happen, we shouldn't have gone there in the first place."

"Never in my wildest dreams," she said, side-eyeing me while keeping her face forward, "did I imagine you would hijack an entire restaurant and do a group healing session."

"Well, spirits can make you go crazy sometimes," I said.

"Is that all you have to say for yourself?" she scoffed. "Your aunt Hilda is so upset."

"Who cares? Even after I delivered messages to more than a hundred people, she still called me a parasite, like I'm some nasty tapeworm that lives in your stomach. I couldn't care less that she's upset."

"Well, that's really too bad," she said, "because your father is going to take you to visit her this weekend so you can apologize in person."

"That's ridiculous," I said. "I'm not sorry. The best I can do for you is write her an e-mail and tell her that I'm sorry she's so offended by me."

She gripped the wheel, her fingers flying up and down in waves, while she took a deep breath. "Baylor Douglas Bosco," she growled, "you will visit your aunt Hilda and you will apologize sincerely to her, or else you will not get your driver's license till you're eighteen."

She had me in a death grip.

"Fine," I said. "Fine, I'll do it, but if you ever make me go to an Italian place again, you better believe it's going to be a hundred times worse than tonight was."

That night I asked Colonel Fleetwood to give me a moment alone with Kristina, and she got an earful.

"Your job is to protect me, Kristina, from all those crazy spirits," I said, my voice firm and tense. She was sitting in my desk chair, staring guiltily, while I paced in front of her. "And you and Colonel Fleetwood were so busy joking with each other that you couldn't even do the one thing you're supposed to. You might as well not have even been there. You might as well have been one of the ghosts crowding around the tables and making noise and distracting me." I shot her a look. "Oh, wait, you *were* one of those ghosts crowding around and distracting me."

"Baylor, I know, I'm sorry," she said. "You just have to understand, it was such a nice change for me to have a friend on this side for once."

"I'm your friend, Kristina. Talk to me."

"Oh, stop, you know what I mean," she said. "A friend who can talk to me instead of having to make weird faces at me."

"Well, that's the way it is!" I said. "There's a reason someone like Colonel Fleetwood isn't usually around, and tonight made it very clear why. You totally failed me. You should have been paying attention to me the entire time instead of letting me down."

"Oh, Baylor," she said, gazing at her feet, "shut up."

I stopped pacing. "What?"

"You heard me. Shut up. Just stop talking." She stood up, walked over to where I was staring at her, dumbfounded, and got in my face. "It must be so hard for you to be alive, and to be surrounded by your family, who can touch you and love you and hug you and kiss you, and it must be such a *challenge* for you not to be able to eat in one certain kind of restaurant, and to talk to anyone you want whenever you want, and to feel the sun in your face and the cold on your skin, and to be able to cry when you're upset and *feel* things."

She paused, her eyes searing into mine. "I am so sorry that you feel so put upon. I apologize for not banishing that creepy guy at the restaurant fast enough, and sure, maybe I shouldn't have let that ghost trick you into thinking he was the waiter, but if that's really the worst I've ever screwed up, then you know what, Baylor? You should just *shut up.*"

And she turned around and disappeared.

I had never gotten into a real fight with Kristina before, and I was fuming. Absolutely fuming. Who did she think she was to talk to me like that? She was the one who'd screwed up, not me. I should have been the one to march away and end the conversation, not her.

It ticked me off big-time, and it was all I could think about at school the next day, especially since Kristina was being petty and didn't make an appearance that morning.

And it was all I could think about that evening, too, which was problematic, since I had plans to go to the Patty Joint downtown with Aiden and J.

Even a trip to the Patty Joint—a rustic restaurant with license plates covering the bare wooden walls, and the home of the best cheeseburgers in New Hampshire—couldn't invigorate my mood.

"What's up with you, Baylor?" J asked between bites of a mozzarella stick. "You've barely said a word all night, and from the looks of it, you seem to have a personal vendetta against that Rhode Island license plate you keep glaring at."

Stupid Rhode Island, with its stupid license plate

covered in blue waves and anchors and the words "Ocean State," as if people really thought of Rhode Island when they thought of oceans.

I shook my head and sighed.

"Sorry, I'm just a little out of it," I said. "Lots on my mind."

"Hmm." She pushed her glasses—tonight's were covered in dark-blue stripes—up the bridge of her nose. "Does this have anything to do with the article?"

"The what?"

She looked down at the mozzarella stick basket. "The article about the boy medium at Carrino's? It's online."

I looked over at Aiden, who seemed very interested in swirling ranch around his plate with his mozzarella stick.

"I haven't read it yet. What'd it say?"

"Oh, it was nothing bad," she said brightly. "If anything, it sounded like it would've been amazing to witness it."

I felt awkward because I'd never really broached the whole ghost subject with J.

I nodded. "Yeah, it was actually kinda cool, minus the old lady I nearly killed, and minus the fact that my mom hates me for ruining my aunt Hilda's birthday dinner."

Aiden choked. "Aunt Hilda? Oh, yikes."

"I know," I said. "Nightmare."

"I'm sure your mom doesn't hate you," J said, whispering. My mom and Mrs. Kirkwood were having a mom date at another table. I'm sure my mom was talking nonstop about last night's escapades.

"I know," I said. "There's just . . . there's some other stuff going on too, and she said she's not going to help me with it, and after last night she's *definitely* not going to help."

"Like what?"

"I need to go to Boston for something."

"What's in Boston?" Aiden asked.

"Just some, uh, ghost stuff I'm trying to figure out." J didn't know about the Sheet Man or my fight with Kristina, and as far as I was concerned, she didn't need to. Things were so out of control that I wanted to keep only a few people in the know, which would hopefully keep everyone else out of danger.

Our burgers arrived, and as I loaded mine with mustard and ketchup, J was staring over my shoulder. I'd seen that look before—the wheels were spinning in her brain.

"Baylor," she said quietly, leaning in, "what if we all took the bus to Boston?"

"Wouldn't it take, like, three hours on the bus?" I

frowned. "Besides, buses aren't exactly my style. Last time I was on one, a tiny Venezuelan woman kept yelling at me about recipes."

"But we'll be there to distract you!" she said, touching Aiden's arm. He immediately started coughing, pulling his hands away and grabbing his napkin to cover his mouth. It usually took him several seconds to recover from unexpected contact with J.

"Totally," he said, his cheeks completely red. "Let's do it."

I looked at them both across from me, their eyes wide and eager, and I smiled.

The next morning I left a note on the kitchen counter, telling my parents I was working on a project with J and to call if they needed me. I was even more proud of the fact that nothing on the note was a lie. It's not like I said I was going to her house, and we *were* working on a project, just one of the ghost variety.

Wearing my backpack, which contained the handy-dandy talisman—just in case—I biked to the bus stop downtown, where J and Aiden were waiting for me already. As I chained my bike, I eavesdropped on their thrilling conversation.

"Dinner was pretty good, huh?" Aiden said.

"So good. I love that place," J said. "Your mom was so sweet to give me a ride."

"Yeah, my mom's great."

"She is. I loved how, uh, excited she got when Baylor delivered that message to the waiter as we were leaving."

I felt like I could hear the blood rushing to Aiden's face. "Uh, yeah, she sure can scream, huh?"

It was like the Italian restaurant fiasco, part two, except not nearly as dramatic. She'd squealed so loud that the everyone in the Patty Joint turned to stare at her. There was no question which side of the family Aiden got his blushing skills from.

"It was cute," J said, her voice gentle and reassuring.

"You guys ready?" I asked as I approached them.

"You bet!" J said, handing me a ticket. "Eight thirty-five bus to Boston. We'll get there at eleven, do some investigating, and get our tickets home on either the three or five p.m. bus."

"Perfect," I said. The bus pulled up a few minutes later, and we were on our way.

The bus ride wasn't that bad, mostly because it was nearly empty. There was only one ghost asking me to pass on a message, and I waited until we arrived in Boston to deliver it.

The worst part of the ride was the very beginning, when we had to pick seats. I sat in a window seat without thinking, realizing too late that I should've arranged for J and Aiden to sit together. Instead I got to watch in horror as Aiden and J stammered to figure out who should sit next to me and who should sit alone.

Ultimately, J sat next to me, and Aiden sat across the aisle, all alone. He made sure to glare at me whenever J wasn't looking.

We took the T to the stop nearest the coffee shop where William Parker apparently worked. I had done some serious online stalking to find the place, a little café called Cup-o'-Soul. He worked there on the weekends, while attending grad school at Boston University. I'd found a research paper he'd written on the criminology department's website.

"We'll be right across the street if you need us," J said, pointing to the other coffee shop.

"Good luck, dude," Aiden said. I nodded to them, thinking about Colonel Fleetwood's comment about running toward death on the battlefield, and marched inside.

14

Things don't always go as planned.

THE CAFÉ WAS PACKED WITH BOLD-COLORED couches and round tables, and the wall behind the baristas was made of exposed brick. Rhythmic New Age music played from hidden speakers. It all felt very cool.

I approached the counter, fully aware that I had no idea what to do.

"Welcome to Cup-o'-Soul," said the frizzy-haired girl behind the cash register. She was short and perky, with teeth so white that she must have used bleach straight from the bottle to brush them. "What can I serve you today?"

"I, uh, I will have a . . . let's go with . . . how about . . ." The barista frowned. "I'll have a macchiato."

"It's mah-*KEE*-ato, not mah-*chee*-ato."

"Totally," I said, nodding. "I'm also looking for someone. William Parker? Does he work here?"

"Will? Yeah, he's on break in the back," she said. "I can get him for you. . . ."

"Please." I nodded.

She disappeared into the back room, and a few moments later she was followed out by a tall, lanky guy with shaggy blond hair. His nose was far too big for his face, and his acne scars resembled the craters of the moon, but just like the girl, he was smiling kindly.

"Can I help you, little dude?"

"Yeah, uh, hi," I said, really wishing for some reason that Kristina were there. "I was wondering if I could speak to you for a few minutes?"

"About what?" he said. His smile never faltered, but his eyes had drooped.

"I really think you should be sitting down for this part," I said, jerking my head to an empty couch near the window.

I grabbed my coffee, which was in a tiny glass, as he circled around the counter, and we sat down on plush purple sofas.

"I'm Baylor Bosco," I said. "And I know you're Will Parker. I took the bus from Keene this morning to see you. You're Alfred's son, right?"

He frowned. "Did you know my dad?"

"Okay, Will, I'm going to be honest with you, and I just need you to hear me out with an open mind."

He didn't say anything, much less react, so I kept going.

"I can communicate with people who've crossed over, so I—"

"Are you trying to tell me you can talk to dead people?"

"That's exactly what I'm telling you."

He rolled his eyes. "You've gotta be kidding me. Do you know how many loons have come out here and tried to tell me my dad left them a message telling me to invest in their company? At least a dozen. So who are you? What are you going to try to sell me on? It's not going to work, but I'm just curious, since you're the youngest one who's tried to do it so far. How old are you? Ten?"

"I'm almost fourteen! And listen, I'm not after your money," I said, spinning the small cup around with my fingers. "I swear. I'm here because I think your dad is in trouble." I took a sip and immediately regretted it. The bitter taste seeped down my throat like Drano.

"How could my dad be in trouble?" Will asked, his voice like acid as he watched me convulse from the coffee. "He's been dead for three years."

"I know that," I said. "But last week he visited me. He was wrapped in a sheet and couldn't speak. All he did was stare at me with these horrible black eyes."

Will stared at me the way most people stare at roadkill. "My dad didn't have black eyes. And if he was in a sheet, how'd you know it was him?"

"He visited a couple more times, and then he finally showed me his shoes. It had to be his way of communicating with me, because I found the exact same pair the next day, and they had his name in them, and then I searched online and found you and your sister."

He scoffed, looking at the frizzy-haired barista and shaking his head. "This is so stupid."

"I know it sounds crazy, but it can't be a coincidence that I just happened to find the exact same pair of shoes that the spirit was wearing, and they just happened to have 'A. Parker' written in them."

"What shoes?" he said, narrowing his eyes.

"They're brown with golden stitching on the sides, and there's a silver buckle on top."

He hesitated. "Those are the shoes he was buried in."

I bit my lip. "I don't mean to sound awkward, but

he wasn't buried in those shoes. Not unless he had two pairs."

He shook his head. "He was buried in those shoes." There was no point in arguing, even if he was totally wrong. We sat in silence for a few seconds, then he pointed at the little cup of brown sewage. "That might taste better if you put some more milk in it. It's on the counter."

I filled it up to the brim with milk and stirred it. It looked sort of like chocolate milk now, so maybe I'd be able to trick myself into thinking it tasted like it too.

When I sat down, Will was mindlessly scratching his upper arm, and I could see a tattoo hidden below the sleeve.

"What's the tattoo?" I asked before taking a sip of the drink.

Nope. Definitely not chocolate milk. I tried not to spit it out.

"Oh, this?" He pushed up his sleeve to reveal three stick figures: one boy and two girls. "It's me, my sister, and my mom."

His father seemed to hang in the air again as we stared at each other awkwardly. There were sugar packets on the table between us, and I thought I'd give the macchiato one last try with some sweetener.

I skimmed my fingers through the packets, looking for one that just said SUGAR, when I felt myself pulled into a memory attached to a packet of SuperSweetz.

It was a quick one: A woman was reaching for a packet of sugar when a red minivan crashed violently into a truck outside the window, and people rushed out of the café to help.

I lurched back to reality, knocking the packets all over the table. "Dang it," I said, gathering them up as he stared at me. "My bad. There was a memory attached to one of the sugars."

"A memory?"

"Yeah," I mumbled. "It happens sometimes, I have no idea how to control it."

"What was it?"

"A minivan hit a truck, and then a bunch of people rushed out to help. Whoever left the memory must have been really shocked. That's usually how it works, some kind of strong feeling behind it."

He blinked at me, bewildered. "That just happened a couple of days ago. It was the loudest bang I've ever heard. Everyone was freaked out."

"Oh," I said, nodding. "Hope no one was hurt."

"Everyone was fine," he said slowly, like he . . . like he didn't know what to think anymore. He was clearly confused that I knew about the accident, and I realized this was my shot to get him talking.

"Would you mind telling me about your dad?" I asked quietly, trying not to sound too desperate. "I'm just trying to figure out what he wants. I'm trying to figure out what he did when he was alive that was so bad."

He was looking at his hands, which were clenched tightly together, and I thought he was going to tell me to shut up. Miraculously, he started talking.

"The man was a machine, Baylor. Super successful. Good shape. Then he married some chick named Angela, got dementia, and left her all his money, and now my sister and I are broke, and there's nothing we can do about it." He looked up at me. "So if it is him, maybe he feels guilty for marrying some greedy, gold-digging monster who dismantled our inheritance, stole it for herself, and left his kids out to dry. Does that answer your question?"

"I'm sorry," I said. "I didn't mean to make you mad."

"It's not your fault, kid," he said, standing up. "I've dealt with it, it's whatever. I've moved on. My sister got out of Dodge, my mom stayed in Winchester, and God knows where Angela went. She didn't even show up to his funeral."

He said her name with an exaggerated Spanish accent, so it sounded like "An-hell-a."

"Maybe that's why he's visiting me?" I suggested, also standing. "Maybe he wants to make it right somehow."

"Do you really think we haven't tried?" he laughed. "We tried, many times. The legal documents were rock solid."

Part of me was panicking. What if the Sheet Man was going to stay with me forever? Will was my best chance at making this whole thing stop. "There has to be something we can do."

"We?" he said. "There's no 'we' here, Baylor. You're just a kid. You're not going to be able to do anything we haven't already tried."

I stood there frowning.

He sighed. "I wish you luck, Baylor," he said. "I really do. I'd love it if you found a way, but I know you won't be able to, so I'm not bothering to offer my help." He turned away and started to walk to the counter. "Cool trick with the sugar, kid."

I lunged over the sofa and grabbed his arm. "Can I at least get your number in case something comes up?"

He sighed. "Fine." He grabbed a napkin, bent over the counter, and scribbled his number. "Here."

"Thanks!" I said. "I'll leave you mine, too, just in case."

"Great," he said, although I strongly suspected he didn't think it was great at all. After he marched away, I went back to the counter, where the barista had been watching us.

"Did you enjoy your macchiato?" she asked.

"Not even a little bit," I said, setting down the still-full glass on the counter and wondering if that awful taste would ever go away. "Could I get a water and maybe some mouthwash if you've got it?"

Across the street Aiden and J were sitting at a table, chatting merrily about Debate Club. J was the president of the club, and Aiden was the worst-performing member. When I sat down, they were debating about what the next topic for the club should be, and Aiden was finishing an impassioned speech about sandwiches.

"I'm telling you, it's the perfect subject," he said, his arms flailing. "Everyone has their own very specific favorite sandwich, with a million different variables, and it's the sign of the truly skilled debater to convince someone why theirs is the best."

J was giggling and shaking her head as she turned to me.

"So how'd it go, Baylor?"

I frowned. I didn't know what I had expected. Maybe

a tearful, grateful son, sharing all his knowledge about his father with me? Maybe an angry person with a clear story as to why his father was most certainly at home in the evil part of the other side?

But what I got from Will wasn't helpful. Leaving your kids no money is pretty bad, but it doesn't make you evil. I still had no real answer for what was happening with his father.

It seemed safer to keep them both in the dark as much as possible about the Sheet Man, so I just told them the practical facts of what Will had told me, and how none of it was very useful.

"Well, that's annoying," J said. "But at least you learned the ex-wife lives in Winchester? Maybe you can visit her next."

I hadn't even thought of that. "Brilliant, J!" I said. "You are *brilliant.*"

"She *is* brilliant," Aiden said dreamily. We both turned to him, and a look of horror dawned on his face that he'd apparently uttered those words aloud.

"Uh, time to go, guys, right?" he said, hopping up. "Let's get a move on."

I'd never seen Aiden move that fast in my life unless a pepperoni sandwich was at stake.

"Wait a second!" J said, looking at her watch. "The next bus to Keene isn't for an hour and a half."

Aiden turned around, slow-motion style, emanating a silent but very real distress signal out to the world, his eyes begging for help from me, from the barista, from a hole in the ground that would swallow him up and take him far away from here.

"What are we going to do for an hour and a half?" he croaked.

"We could do some sightseeing?" I suggested. "Anything close to here?"

"It's Boston!" J said, her eyes bulging with excitement. "The birthplace of the American Revolution. There's *so* much to see. We could walk part of the Freedom Trail and visit the key sites of the Revolution! The Boston Massacre, the Old State House, Paul Revere's house, and oh, I think Paul Revere's grave is on the trail too. You might like that, Baylor!"

"Uh," I said, horrified by my mistake. "I think the river's nearby. Can we just go look at that?"

"Look at the river?" She looked bewildered, turning her head back and forth from me to Aiden. "But all the stuff I just . . . oh, come on, guys, you at least have to see the Boston Tea Party ships!" She smiled eagerly at Aiden, but he didn't notice, since he was still mentally berating himself.

"Sure," I said. "Is it on the river, right over there, steps away?"

She frowned. "No."

"Darn," I said, picking up my bag. "To the river!"

We crossed Storrow Drive and wound up on an embankment along the river. It was freezing—the wind was blasting like a high-speed train over the river, apparently arriving fresh from the Arctic Circle.

"Isn't this great?" I said, teeth clattering, to J, who was clutching her arms over her chest. "What a view." The river was a dark, choppy mess; the sky was gray and bleak.

"Yeah, Baylor," J said sarcastically, "this was your best idea ever."

Aiden, still too afraid to say anything, stood motionless, looking like he wanted nothing more than for the wind to pick him up and carry him swiftly away.

"Let's just go," J said. "We'll get to the bus station early and have some hot chocolate."

I set my backpack down and took a step closer to the concrete balustrade on the edge of the river. "You want to leave already? We just got here."

"You've got thirty more seconds until I kick you into the river," she said between shivers.

I looked out at the gray sky; there was such a thick layer of clouds blocking the sun that it felt like a miracle the light was making its way through at all. I remembered the nonsense that Kristina and the colonel said when we made the talisman, about the sun knowing only light, so the moon's light in the darkness was more special. I scoffed. What did they know? Look at the sun now, doing its best to shove its rays through the nearly impenetrable Boston sky.

A prickle of chills lightly spread on the back of my neck, a different sort of cold than what we'd been experiencing.

"Baylor, let's go!" J said defiantly. "I've had enough."

"One second," I said, leaning far over the railing, the concrete hard against my stomach. There was something there, some kind of presence. I could feel it.

Any color that had been in the sky seemed to disappear.

I turned to look at J and Aiden, but they were gone. The chill in my neck now pulsated throughout my body, and I swung back around to face the river.

Over the violent waters the Sheet Man was gliding right toward me.

TIP

15

Seriously,
DO NOT PANIC.

THE EYES WERE FOCUSED ON ME, UNBLINK-
ing, little black holes soaking up light and energy. The
sheet was perfectly still despite its quick movement
through the fierce wind and thrashing waves.

The talisman! It was in my bag steps away.

I crawled off the railing, dismayed to see I was
totally alone. J, Aiden, all the other pedestrians that
had been walking by—were they really gone, or was
Alfred transporting me to some other realm, some
sort of perpetual limbo where only he existed?

I lunged for my bag, but before I had the chance

to unzip it, the Sheet Man was there, so close I could reach out and touch him. My breathing became shallow and I felt light-headed. This was it. He'd finally gotten me. I noticed the shoes were gone, so his bare feet hung there, the toenails yellow and shriveled.

And the eyes. I looked back at the feet because the eyes were scarier than I remembered, especially this close up, like ash was smeared around them.

"Can I help you, Alfred?" I asked, clutching the bag, sneakily attempting to open it, trying to keep my voice from shaking.

No response.

"I met your son today. William? He was disappointed in you."

Still nothing. He just floated there like a casual ghost friend of mine. He didn't seem to notice my hand inching into the bag.

"He said you didn't leave him or your daughter any inheritance. You left all your money to your new wife."

I'd struck a nerve. A strange scream erupted from somewhere inside of him, and then, like he was giving birth to another evil Sheet Man, a spirit hurtled out from under the sheet. It was tangled in the fabric, the arms tied up like they were handcuffed. The spirit unraveled itself, and I gasped.

"Kristina!" I yelled, dropping the bag. "What the . . . how the . . ."

"Baylor!" she yelled. "The wife! Talk to the—"

And then they disappeared.

At the same moment Aiden and J came back into focus, screaming my name over the railing by the river.

"I'm here," I shouted behind them. I noticed they were no longer alone; people had stopped to help them.

"How did you do that?" J yelled, running over to me, Aiden hot on her heels, tears streaming down their faces. "You disappeared"—she snapped her fingers—"like that."

I was barely paying attention to them. How could I? Kristina was caught in whatever limbo the Sheet Man existed, and there was nothing I could do about it.

"It was like an alien beamed you up," Aiden said, bending over, huffing loudly.

"It was him," I said, my voice hoarse. "The father of the guy I visited today. And he somehow took Kr—another ghost hostage." I swallowed, the lump in my throat huge, the tears seconds away. I was too afraid to say her name out loud. What if it somehow affected her? "I . . . I don't know what to do. This situation is absurd. They're all dead. There's no one I can call. There's no one I can turn to." I looked at their tearstained faces, and I wondered if they were somehow in danger just being around me.

Where was Colonel Fleetwood? Surely, he had to be aware of Kristina's absence. Unless he had been kidnapped too?

"I need to go home," I said. "I need to light a million candles."

Before I knew what was happening, a gruff pair of hands turned me around.

"You gave your friends quite a scare there, son." A police officer was looking me up and down. He'd walked over from the river, and I noticed an ambulance was pulling up behind him. "They thought you'd fallen into the river."

I turned to Aiden. "You called nine-one-one?"

Aiden raised his hands limply. "We didn't know what to do, Baylor. We thought you were drowning."

"Luckily, I was nearby and could offer my help," the officer said, puffing out his chest. "Your parents around, son?"

I gulped. A chill entirely unrelated to the Sheet Man or the cold entered the pit of my stomach. "We live in Keene."

"You kids are in Boston alone?"

"We took the bus," J said.

"I see," he said. "Looks like I'm going to have to give them a call."

"That won't be necessary, Officer," I said, brushing myself off and gathering up my bag. "Really, I'm fine, and we have a bus to catch."

"You three are minors alone in Boston who just had to call nine-one-one because one of you nearly went tumbling over the river's edge." He smiled kindly but spoke firmly. "What's your parents' phone number, son?"

My mom spoke to the officer at length, and when he handed the phone to me, she tersely said two sentences before hanging up: "Take the bus home. I'll pick you up at the station."

J, Aiden, and I didn't say a word to one another the entire ride home. They knew I was furious with them for calling the cops, but they also felt completely justified in trying to save my life.

When we got to the bus station, my mom was there with a nervous-looking Mrs. Kirkwood.

"J, Mrs. Kirkwood is going to take you home," my mom said, not looking at me. She turned to Aiden's mom. "I'll call you later, Karen." She marched to the car, and I looked one last time at Aiden and J. It was obvious I was a dead man walking; their smiles, meant to be encouraging, looked more like Ella's when we tried to feed her pureed peas.

"Not a word," my mom said, her voice a dangerous whisper. "Not one word until we're home." Of course. She and Dad had to yell at me together.

My mom may have wanted to make sure my dad was present to yell at me, but she took care of the bulk of it herself.

"I forbade you, Baylor," she said, chopping away at a bunch of carrots. I could imagine her hanging up the phone with the officer and heading straight to the store to stock up in preparation of this exact moment. "I literally said, 'I am forbidding you to go.' Let that word soak in for a second. Forbid."

She chopped as I sat at the kitchen table in silence. My dad sat next to me. He didn't seem angry as much as he was abysmally confused.

"*Forbid.* And why did I forbid it, Baylor? Do you remember?"

I didn't say anything. If there was one thing I knew about my mom, it was that it was best to let her get it all out, no matter how long it took, like a balloon slowly, painfully deflating its air.

"Because you told me you wanted to meet the son

of that dead thing that put you in the hospital. Now,
that's just crazy, isn't it? Isn't it, Douglas?"

My dad grunted.

"I thought it sounded like a bad idea, Baylor,
because you could get hurt, maybe wind up in the
hospital again, something awful." She heaved a pile
of diced carrots into a Tupperware container. "And
then today I get a *phone call* from a *police officer* in *Boston*
about my son, who was there alone with friends and
seemed to go missing, and guess what, Baylor. *You
proved that it was a bad idea.*"

It went on like that for a while, until they sent
me to my room to begin my punishment of being
grounded for forever, and then when they died and
crossed over, they were still going to make sure I was
grounded. I never gave them a straight answer about
what led Aiden and J to call the police, nor did I tell
them the Sheet Man made another appearance, this
time with Kristina in tow. I didn't ever plan to tell
them, since my mom would go berserk.

Seriously, what was I going to do? Whenever I had
a question, I turned to Kristina. Kristina was the one
who was supposed to stick with me. She was the one
who was supposed to protect me from the evil spirits,
especially the demons, like the Insymbios, who could
sneak in unnoticed, take over my body, and make me

go insane; or even worse, the Bru—I stopped and took a deep breath, vanquishing the thought from my brain. Even thinking about them could make me vulnerable.

What could I do to protect her? I couldn't bounce between realms. I couldn't simply walk over to the Beyond and ask for help. Even if I could go to the Beyond, which I obviously couldn't access since I wasn't dead, I wouldn't know what to say. The Sheet Man seemed to exist in his own weird, lifeless limbo, and it wasn't like I'd be able to cough up directions on how to reach him.

My mom was right. It was chaos on the other side.

With candles lit, I demanded Colonel Fleetwood get his butt back over here so we could come up with a plan.

Nothing. Not even a creak in the floor. Not even a flicker of the lights. Not any sort of small sign that anyone or anything was listening to me.

If Kristina was my buffer to the other side, it was horrifyingly possible that with her taken out of the loop, I'd lost my "in" with the Beyond. Could that really be?

My little séance obviously wasn't working, so I hopped on my computer and searched for Alfred's wife. Kristina's one clue was my only solid lead. But Angela was nowhere to be found.

Then I remembered that the ex-wife lived in Winchester, and J had suggested I find her next. She could be easy to track down, and maybe she knew something.

Sure enough, Rosalie Parker's address was listed online; she was located just outside of Winchester's little downtown area.

I jotted the address onto a piece of paper and ran downstairs.

"Dad, we're going into Winchester tomorrow, right? I need to apologize to Aunt Hilda and everything."

He and my mom both turned to me with shocked expressions.

"Baylor Bosco, what do you have planned?" my mom asked, her eyes narrowing.

"Nothing!" I said. "I just feel really bad about everything."

"Fine by me," my dad said with a shrug. "I want to stop at that fishing store on Main Street too."

"Well, be sure to call Aunt Hilda before you head down there," Mom said scathingly. "We don't want you to surprise her and give her a heart attack."

After a sleepless night, the next morning couldn't come fast enough. Luckily, my dad was an early riser because of his job, so we both got ready and drove the thirty minutes to Winchester. We ate breakfast at a café on Main Street, where he tried to talk to me about my fiascos in Boston and at Aunt Hilda's birthday dinner.

"Between you and me, I think it's crazy your mom is making you apologize to her," he said between bites of his ham-and-cheese omelet. "I walked into that place knowing something was going to happen. Everyone knows you can't function properly in Italian restaurants."

"*Thank you,*" I said, finally feeling vindicated. "Agreed. There were just so many people inside one little space. I sort of lost my mind."

"That being said, it was wrong of you to go to Boston after she *forbade* you from going." It sounded like he'd rehearsed this. "You're going to be paying for that one for a while."

"I know. Again, I'm very sorry."

He sipped his juice and sighed. "I do not envy you, son. The ghosts and the crazy stuff and all." He smiled at me. "Oh, and don't tell your mom I said any of that stuff about Aunt Hilda."

Afterward we browsed the tackle shop. My dad was looking for fall sales to stock up for spring, and he bought a couple of snagless sinkers as well as a few spools of line. But when we called Aunt Hilda at ten to let her know we wanted to come over, she was nowhere near ready.

"Now what?" my dad asked. He looked around at the other shops. "I guess we can get some Christmas shopping done. My mom would probably like something from one of those antique shops."

I shuddered. Antique stores are the worst place for objects with memories attached to them.

"Hey, Dad, you know what? One of my teachers lives just around the corner," I said. "Would you mind driving me over so I could stop by and say hi?"

"You want to visit a teacher on a Sunday at ten a.m.? Isn't that a little weird?" he asked.

"Uh, I don't know, we were almost like friends, this teacher and I."

"Which teacher is it?"

"Mrs. Parker. Remember her? She's divorced now."

He scrunched his face together as he thought. "I don't think so?"

"Come on, it'll only take a few minutes."

"But you're grounded." I could see the wheels spinning in his head, calculating whether or not visiting a teacher really fell into grounded territory. "Why not? I don't mind catching up with my students, I'm sure she won't mind either."

And a few minutes later I was walking up the brick pathway to a tiny brick cottage. I had told my dad to stay in the car, but that he could come say hi at the end if he wanted, which was another bald-faced lie, but whatever.

The house had a nice front porch, with white iron lattice railings around the perimeter. The garden was kept up nicely, which is the universal sign that the homeowners care about their house, and I felt satisfied Rosalie wouldn't answer the door drunk and covered in weeks-old bits of food.

I rang the doorbell and heard a couple of dogs barking. They sounded like big dogs, and I wondered how they liked being cooped up in such a small house.

The door opened, revealing a woman wearing a red bathrobe. Her graying brunette hair was tied up in a ponytail, and she was already wearing makeup. She was pretty and seemed delicate, and I could easily see my mom looking similar to her in twenty years.

"Can I help you?" she asked, her brow furrowed.

"I'm Baylor Bosco, and I can communicate with people who have crossed over," I said. "I was hoping I could speak with you for a few moments about your ex-husband, Alfred."

She shook her head in her surprise, blinking vigorously.

"Is this a joke?"

"I'm sorry," I said. "I know Alfred has been dead for several years, but I've just started receiving very strange visits from him. He won't speak with me, though, so I don't know how to help him."

Her face sort of collapsed. One second she looked normal, the next second everything was wrinkled and twisted.

"You need to go," she said, reaching to close the door.

"No!" I growled, slamming it back open and surprising myself with my sudden fury. "I know he didn't leave your children any money, and now I need to know how to fix it so he'll leave me alone. Where can I find Angela?"

Rosalie was stronger than she looked. She managed to begin closing the door, while staring at me like she wanted to reach down my throat, pull out my intestines, and use them to decorate her Christmas tree. "I don't like to talk about my ex-husband," she said in a voice that wasn't her own. "Get off my property."

The door clicked shut, followed by a massive deadbolt clunk. I stared, stunned. Then I spun around and walked down the path, just as my dad was getting out of the car.

"What happened, Baylor?" He looked shocked.

"Did you make her mad somehow? Bring up the divorce or something?"

"No," I said, "she just didn't remember me. Guess we weren't as close as I thought."

I was so distracted by everything that had happened in the last twenty-four hours—talking to Will, discovering Kristina got ghostnapped, and meeting Rosalie—that I could barely remember why I was at Aunt Hilda's place.

"Sorry I ruined your birthday," I said flatly. "I didn't mean to ruin it. I know you only turn eighty-eight once, and since it was probably your last birthday, I feel bad it didn't go the way you wanted it to."

"Baylor!" my dad exclaimed, trying to force a laugh, while Aunt Hilda's eyes widened to the size of half-dollar coins. "Why don't you try that again?"

"Try what again?"

"Your apology," he said through gritted teeth. "One more time."

"Uh, I'm sorry you don't believe I have the ability to talk to ghosts, even though your friend Marjorie is standing behind you and telling you she's sorry she never paid you the forty bucks you won playing Bunco with her."

"I always thought she cheated," Marjorie said,

shrugging, her voice low and gravelly from what must have been decades of chain-smoking. "Who's that good at Bunco?"

"Marjorie?" Aunt Hilda said. "I just saw Marjorie last night. She can't be dead."

My dad's jaw dropped, and I pressed my lips together.

"Oh, sorry, kid," Marjorie said, laughing. "Forgot to mention I'm fresh as of early this morning."

"Thanks a lot, Marge," I snapped, looking at the troublemaking ghost over Aunt Hilda's shoulder before turning my attention back to her. "Sorry, Aunt Hilda, looks like Marjorie crossed over this morning."

Aunt Hilda looked at me with indecipherable eyes, and then she caustically spit, "I don't believe you."

"She's in for a nasty surprise if no one finds me before my cats run out of food," Marjorie said.

I grimaced, but before I could say anything, my dad grabbed my shoulder and steered me out of the apartment. "Sorry, Aunt Hilda. I'll have Connie call you later."

16

Always keep chocolate handy.

NEEDLESS TO SAY, MY MOM WAS NOT HAPPY with me.

"Less than a day after your Boston escapades, you go over to Aunt Hilda's to apologize," she said, her voice low and emotionless, "and you wind up not only telling her that she's not going to have another birthday, but that one of her best friends just died?"

"How was I supposed to know Marjorie had just died?" I said, throwing my hands up. "It's not like the ghosts walk around with a little calendar tied around their neck telling me when they crossed over."

"And not only did you scar your great-aunt, your father seems equally traumatized."

My dad had burrowed himself into a bunch of blankets on the sofa because the experience with Marjorie and Aunt Hilda had resurfaced the memory of me telling him about his father.

"This is not my fault," I said. "None of it is! Be mad at the universe, or God, or Buddha, or Zeus, or whoever you want to be mad at for giving me this gift, but don't be mad at me. I can't help it."

She shook her head, looking sad and defeated. "Can't Kristina help you more? Can't she help you just, I don't know, somehow make them stop? Set up some healing hours and say that you're available to heal only on Saturdays between eleven and three?"

My jaw tensed. "I'll see what she can do."

That night I cracked open my Halloween candy and hunted for anything with chocolate. All the sweet, sugary stuff, like Smarties and Starburst and Skittles, got tossed aside. It was an old habit based on something Kristina said to me once. She had been watching me eat chocolate one day, and in a pathetic, puppy-dog way she said, "The one food I wish I could eat is chocolate. It's brown and strange-looking, but people get so happy when they eat it."

"People get happy eating anything when they're really hungry," I said.

"But chocolate is different. Chocolate is what people get for special occasions. People go out of their way to eat it, even if they're not hungry. Whenever people die suddenly, they never cross over and say, 'I'm so thrilled I decided to eat that stalk of celery.' It's always, 'I'm just happy I decided to eat that last piece of chocolate cake.'"

Since then I've always savored my chocolate, because even though I'm pretty sure I'm not going to die for a while, there's always a chance it could be my last time eating it.

As I chewed on a fun-size Milky Way, I wondered where Kristina was. I wondered whether she was uncomfortable being tied up with the Sheet Man, or if it even bothered her at all. It was probably just a minor inconvenience. It probably felt like only a couple of hours had passed. I was worried for her, of course, but I couldn't help but feel defeated by the fact that she was already dead. In books, TV shows, and movies the main drama always seems to involve death somehow, and how terrible it is.

Death was the least of my concerns. What more could the Sheet Man do to her, really? He could keep her trapped in that weird dimension he existed in. He could replace her eyes with black buttons to make her look like him. He could convert her to the Sheet Woman and make Sheet Babies. I shuddered. That was a terrifying thought.

I wanted to panic about her being gone, but all I could think about was how her absence affected *me*. Her duty was to assist me, and now that she was missing, it meant that a very important piece of my daily life was gone.

I swallowed the candy and reached for another as it dawned on me that this sort of thinking was the reason she had snapped at me that night after the Italian dinner. I was so worried about myself and how she could help me that I rarely thought about her.

But . . . she was dead! There was really nothing I could do to help her, and if she'd been having ghostly feelings about loneliness and missing out on the human experience, then she should have mentioned them rather than lashing out.

Right? That was a reasonable request. It was just hard to imagine her as a real person with feelings, but maybe I needed to do that nowadays. Her world was just so different from mine. Sure, we spent the majority of my waking hours together, but when I slept, Kristina was off in the Beyond living her secretive ghost life. I had no idea what happened over there except for the half hints and clues she gave me.

I sighed and grabbed yet another Milky Way. None of this would matter if she never got out of Sheet Man limbo. But I would get her out. I had the talisman. The Sheet Man would visit me again, and I would stop him and get Kristina back.

My phone rang suddenly, interrupting my thoughts. I didn't recognize the area code, but I picked up anyway, secretly hoping Kristina had somehow used her energy to communicate via the phone.

"Hello?"

"Hi, is this Baylor?"

"Uh, yes, hi. Who's this?"

"My name is Isabella Parker."

I shot up and jumped to my desk.

"Isabella!" I said. "I didn't expect to hear from you."

"Will told me about your meeting yesterday," she said. "It sounded pretty awkward."

"Yeah, he didn't seem too eager to speak with me."

"You probably caught him off guard," she said. "To be honest, I was caught off guard too. But then I searched for you online and came across all sorts of information. Did you know you have fans, Baylor? There are a couple of websites devoted to you. One group calls themselves the Baylievers."

I was thankful she couldn't see me blush. "That's

embarrassing. I really don't Google myself too often."

"And I found an article about you from just the other day. Apparently, you knocked over a lady and then held an impromptu reading at an Italian restaurant?"

"That . . . that, yes, that happened, but it was all an accident."

"Whatever it was, it's amazing to read about, and I called you the instant I read the last word."

"Well, thanks, I guess. It'll be helpful to learn more about your father."

"Will told me Dad's visiting you and wears a sheet on his head the whole time? That's very unlike him. He was a social creature and wouldn't hide himself like that."

"Could he have been involved with some bad deeds in his life?" I asked. "Maybe some dark stuff you don't know about?"

"I doubt it," she said, speaking a little faster. "He was a great guy. Even toward the end, when he had his memory problems, he was so sweet and felt so bad when he forgot one of us."

"Isabella, his presence is shrouded in evil," I said. "Something's wrong with this picture."

"It's got to be something with Angela." She said the

name in the same exaggerated accent as her brother. "That woman! She was evil, Baylor. She probably did something to my dad, and the residue of it is affecting his afterlife."

"What could she have done that was so bad?"

"Well, for starters, she only married the man for his money!" she said exuberantly, and I could picture her shaking her fist on the other end of the phone. "She was less than half his age when they got married, and they had dated for only a few months. It was so obvious! And then when he died, to find out that he'd left her all the money and didn't leave a dime for us? I don't buy it. She knew exactly what she was doing."

"It still doesn't explain the sheet," I said. "I can communicate just fine with people who've done far worse things."

"I don't think she was treating him right," she said. "Toward the end, whenever we visited them at their home, something felt . . . off. And I'm not just saying that because I don't like her."

"I don't know," I said. "It still doesn't seem serious enough for him to deserve this sort of fate."

"Then Angela must have done something worse, and we don't know about it," she said.

"Do you know where I could find her? To ask her some questions?"

"No idea," she said. "Once my dad died, she disappeared. She recently had the estate sale, so I bet she's gearing up to sell the house and run off with even more money."

"I hope not," I said. "That sort of bad karma catches up with everyone eventually."

"God, Baylor, this all makes sense in a weird way," she said. "I've never felt my dad's presence in the years since he died. Not once, not even so much as a nightmare with him in it. It's like a void."

"Well, hopefully, we'll be able to fix that soon."

"I hope so," she said. "I really do."

We ended the chat with the promise to call each other should we learn anything more. I hung up and looked at the notes I had written down on my notepad.

Nothing. It was nice of her to call, but I got nothing concrete from her.

I sighed and lay back down on my bed. I was no closer to finding Kristina than before.

When we were kids, we'd get into such trouble sometimes. Well, I'd get into trouble, and she'd giggle on the other side. Having a clued-in dead sister as an accomplice was not good for my behavior. One time at school Kristina told me the code to get into the teachers' lounge, and I sneaked in and took some sodas. I did it a couple of times more, and then I got cocky and brought some friends with me. As we were raiding the fridge, a teacher caught us and marched us straight down to the principal's office, where all my friends promptly turned me in as the ringleader.

Imagine explaining to your principal that your invisible sister gave you the code and you didn't realize it would get you in trouble. That led to a couple of awkward meetings with my parents, and afterward they gave me the strict instructions never to mention my gift to anyone.

This was all before Kristina went away and learned more about her soul's purpose. After that she rarely goofed around at all. But I still thought of us as partners in crime, and the fact that I didn't know how to help her like she'd helped me a million times before was the only thing on my mind as I tossed and turned that night.

17

Try not to miss the obvious.

I DREAMED I WAS WALKING THROUGH THE cemetery and saw Tommy Thorne. He was standing under the giant tree, guarding his tombstone, his bright red hoodie shrouded in mist. When he saw me, he tilted his head, his jet-black hair sweeping to the side.

"You know where to find peace," he said.

Then I woke with a start, unsure of when I'd fallen asleep in the first place.

It was seven forty-five on Monday morning, and I'd overslept big-time. I sprinted to the shower, rinsed off, brushed my teeth, and got dressed all in about three minutes.

Downstairs my mom was bouncing Ella on her hip.

"You're still here?" she said. "I thought you left twenty minutes ago."

"Obviously not," I said, grabbing a banana and heading out the door.

"Stay out of trouble," she called as I shut the door.

It was too late for that. The street was swarmed with spirits. Did Kristina really block that many out for me? There hadn't been that many out yesterday, though, so that couldn't be it. I walked down the block toward school, pulling my hoodie over my head and keeping my eyes to the ground.

It's always disconcerting to see demons floating around that early in the morning, and I felt strangely vulnerable without Kristina there to act as my buffer and, as much as I hated to admit it, my security blanket. Even though the spirits weren't bothering me that morning, all I wanted was to go straight to the cemetery. Tommy clearly had a message for me, and I needed to hear it. Maybe it would help me get a step closer to finding Kristina.

Once I got to school, I realized I hadn't done my routine. I was so zonked out from thinking about Kristina and Tommy and rushing for school that I

completely forgot to surround myself with positive
energy. I ruffled through my bag, pulled out my
emergency lighter, sparked the flame, and enveloped
myself with light, immediately feeling better . . . until
someone screamed my name.

"Baylor Bosco!"

I turned around to look for the source of
anger and saw my vice-principal standing near the
entranceway, glaring at me. Mr. Connell was a very
thin man who wore clothes that were always too
baggy for his body, like dress shirts that were trying
to swallow him whole. His voice also happened to
sound just like Kermit the Frog's.

"What do you think you're doing with that lighter?
Come here, young man."

I imagined a small amphibian scolding me, and I
laughed as I walked up to him.

"Oh, you think it's funny, do you?"

"No, Mr. Connell, I'm sorry, it's all a misunder-
standing."

"I don't think so," he said. "I saw you hold your
lighter close to your face. You know there's no smoking allowed on school property, not to mention the
fact that you're only thirteen! I'm going to have to
search your belongings."

I thought about my mom's words as I'd left the

house: *Stay out of trouble.* Clearly, she was still mad at me, and the last thing I needed was for the school to call her and get me into more trouble.

"Mr. Connell, you read the newspaper, right?"

"What?"

"Did you happen to see that article about me the other day?"

His whole body reacted to my words. His face scrunched, his arms stiffened, and his feet shuffled several times.

"I don't like all that funny business," he said. "Go to class and don't let me catch you doing anything like that again."

I pressed my lips together to smile unpleasantly at him and then slipped past the doors, thankful it hadn't escalated into something further. It always amused me to see how people reacted to my gift. Even after hearing all the rumors and reading the occasional article on it, some people couldn't help but feel skeptical.

As I was walking between first and second periods with one of my band friends, my arm got pulled backward, and I swung around to see J holding on to me with a death grip.

"Hey," I said, rubbing my shoulder. "Everything all right?"

"No, everything's not all right," she said. "Do you

know who Andrew Vallario is?"

The name brought a blurry image of a preppy-looking guy who looked like he brushed his hair a thousand times every night before going to bed.

"I think I've heard of him," I said. "Isn't he almost as smart as you?"

"Yes," she said. "And do you know what he did this morning? He asked me to go to the Fall Ball with him."

My eyes widened for a second as I thought of Aiden's unrequited love for J, then I realized I wasn't playing it cool and regained my composure. But it was too late.

"I knew it!" she said, bouncing on her toes. "Your eyes just gave it all away! Aiden wants to ask me, right?"

"I—I—I can't say," I stuttered.

"You're his best friend! Of course you can!"

"I think it could possibly be something he might have thought about considering?"

"Oh, really helpful, Baylor," she said. "I know Aiden wants to go with me. We spent so much time with each other this weekend, and I don't know how many more hints I can drop before I wind up accidentally asking him myself."

For a second I wondered whether she should just ask him herself. It would save Aiden a lot of awkwardness, and he wouldn't have to panic anymore about whether or not she liked him. But J obviously wasn't going to do that. She might be scarily smart, but she was still a girl who wanted to get asked on a date to the dance.

"Listen, I'll say something to him," I said. "Things are just sort of crazy right now."

"I know, I know," she said. "And I feel bad about even mentioning this to you after what happened on Saturday." She looked at me sadly. "I just don't want to hurt Aiden."

She walked away, her short hair bobbing up and down with every step.

When I recounted the story to Aiden at lunch, he looked like he was about to cry.

"Baylor," he whispered, his voice hoarse and his face a sickly pallor. "I did something really stupid."

"What is it?" I said, thrilled to have something other than Kristina to think about.

"Well, so, after your accident in the band room, Cassie could see I was pretty shaken up about the whole thing. She talked with me for a while after you'd gone to the hospital."

"Cassie who plays the clarinet? Okay. Why does that matter?"

"Well, we kept talking, and we started texting, and

I mean, it was stupid stuff, I thought we were just being friendly. . . ."

"Oh, no, Aiden, please don't say what you're about to say," I said, my hands squeezing my skull.

"She brought the dance up first! And I said it would be fun to go, but I didn't mean with her, I was thinking of J the entire time. But then she must have thought I meant *with her*, and she said yes and that she couldn't wait to go with me, and it all happened before I knew what was even happening!"

"And you didn't immediately tell me?"

"It just happened yesterday," he said, looking forlornly at his sandwich. "I'm still processing it."

"I don't know what to say," I said. "Clarinet Cassie? What were you thinking?"

"I wasn't!" Tears were actually welling up in his eyes. "I think I'm going to be sick."

"Well, you've got to get out of it," I said. "Tell her your phone was stolen and some jerk's been pranking her."

"I can't do that," he said. "I saw her this morning. She was skipping, Baylor. Skipping. You can't reject a girl after you made her so happy that she skips."

"Demon dung," I said, shaking my head. "You're right."

"What'd you just say?" His eyes narrowed in confusion.

"Nothing!" I sputtered, alarmed I'd said Kristina's favorite phrase so casually. "I just feel bad for you." He shrugged, and I could tell he was genuinely distraught. He hadn't even touched his pepperoni sandwich.

"What am I going to do? Once J finds out about Cassie, she's going to hate me and say yes to Andrew and my life will officially be over."

"We'll figure it out," I said. "Don't panic yet. There's got to be a way out of this."

I wished Kristina were there to help. She would've been the perfect person—uh, ghost—to construct a plan.

Aiden spent the rest of the school day texting me stressed messages.

AIDEN: How could I have been so dumb?

AIDEN: What if j finds out?

AIDEN: I ruined my 1 shot at love!!!! :'(

I felt bad for the kid, but no good ideas had sprung to mind, and all my mental energy was focused on finding some way to rescue Kristina.

After band practice I walked the thirty minutes to Woodland Cemetery and went straight to Tommy's

grave. I leaned against it, staring at the swaying spruce
overhead.

"Tommy?" I called out. "Are you around?"

"Right here," said a voice to my left. He was leaning against his mom's tombstone, his hair brushing
the stone, and staring at the spruce just like I was.
"Nice of you to let me through this time."

Someone was a little bitter about being blocked on
Halloween.

"Sorry about that," I said. "I was a little freaked
out that night."

"It's okay," he said. "I know." Tommy mainly
spent his time in the Beyond, but he came back
every now and then to deliver a message or just to
talk to me.

"Thanks for visiting me last night," I said. "I
guess you knew I needed it."

"I could sense your angst. I thought maybe Kristina
hadn't been around to help you for a few days."

"She got taken, Tommy," I said. "The Sheet Man
who attacked me on Halloween night somehow took
her. I've been trying to figure out how to get her back,
but I have no idea how. She's trapped in some sort of
weird limbo dimension."

"That explains why I haven't seen her," he said.

"You guys see each other?"

"Usually, yeah," he said. "Whenever she's in the Beyond."

"What have the ghosts been saying in the Beyond?" I asked, trying not to sound too anxious. "Why haven't they come back to this side to help me out?"

"They might be worried the same thing that happened to her could happen to them."

"But you cross back and forth just fine."

"I'm not one of your spirit guides, though," he said. "Just a friend."

"So the spirit guides have some kind of target on their backs?"

"It's possible, Baylor, but then again, you and Kristina are a special duo. Kristina may be dead, but she's not exactly your average ghost, either."

"What do you mean?" I asked. "She's just . . . a ghost."

"I'm not permitted to say too much," he said, pushing his hair out of his face. Was that some kind of phrase all ghosts were required to learn? "But come on, haven't you ever noticed that Kristina ages with you, while the other ghosts stay the age they died?"

It felt like he'd slapped me. How could I have missed something so obvious? The ghost children running through my dreams that stayed children. The dead grandparents that always stayed grandparents. And even Tommy, the skinny ghost with the cool hair, was still the permanent epitome of cool at age eleven.

But Kristina had been a baby with me, then a toddler, then a walking and talking little kid, and now a teenager. How had I never thought to ask about that?

"You should see your face right now," Tommy said.

"I can't believe I never realized it," I said. "It just seemed . . . natural."

"Of course it did," he said, shrugging.

"So Kristina's special in the Beyond just like I'm special in the physical world?"

He nodded.

"And because of that I'm on my own now?"

"You're never on your own, Baylor," he said, chuckling. "You just can't see or hear how you're being helped like you usually can, which means you're just like everyone else in the physical world."

"Well, I don't like it."

"Maybe you should try something different, then."

"What do you mean?"

"Well, you can't cross into the Beyond because you're still alive, but it seems like you can enter whatever dimension the Sheet Man exists in, right?"

"Right?"

"Well, then . . . enter it."

"You're making it sound so easy, Tommy. How can I get there?"

"Visit another one of your kind and have them help you."

"You think another gifted person could help me?"

He shrugged. "Why not?"

I didn't think Tommy's advice was bad, but I wasn't exactly friends with any other gifted people around town. To be honest, I wasn't sure if there *were* any other legit ones. Kristina had never spoken of any, so I didn't know whether or not to believe in them.

I searched the Internet for a few suggestions, and nearly all the results for Keene turned up with my name somewhere in them. My cheeks burned as I skipped past the Baylievers' fan boards ("Has boy wonder Baylor Bosco helped you somehow? Share your story here!").

But there were a few businesses listed in the area—in Keene, Winchester, some of the surrounding towns, and the mother ship in Boston—and as I perused the websites featuring shiny crystal balls and bloody tarot cards and floating feathers, I couldn't help but understand why people didn't believe in my ability. These people seemed ridiculous. I didn't need any special items to communicate. Sure, a candle helped me with my focus, but I didn't *need* it for my gift to work.

I wrote down the addresses for the two closest shops, both located in downtown Keene, and stuffed the paper into my backpack, next to my talisman. A flash of panic hit me about how I was going to get there. My parents would eviscerate me if they found out I'd gone to visit these shops. I'd just have to skip band practice tomorrow, and as long as I was home in time for dinner, and as long as I evaded any run-ins with the hospital or the police, they'd never need to know.

18

Grandpa
knows best.

THE NEXT DAY SCHOOL PASSED BY IN A flurry of awkward exchanges and glances.

J pointedly glared at me as she walked down the hall with her would-be date, Andrew. He was taller than I remembered, but every bit as preppy. He was wearing a pink button-down and a blue winter vest, and based on his hair, he most likely owned several hundred shares of stock in his favorite pomade company.

Mr. Connell seemed to be following me around the halls, looking for any trace of another lighter.

The third time I spotted him staring at me, I waved at him, and he turned the other direction and marched away like nothing had happened.

Aiden looked like a toddler lost in the mall. First I saw him staring helplessly at me while Cassie chatted merrily to him, and then during lunch he picked at his sandwich and formed sad pepperoni faces with the globs of mustard.

"What happened to the pepperoni?" Bobby asked as he sat down. "They know they're about to be in your stomach or something? Oh, maybe they're thinking about what happens next."

Aiden scowled. "These pepperoni slices are going through a hard time, Bobby."

Bobby blinked at him. "I'm sorry to hear that."

When school ended, I grabbed Aiden and told him to cover for me in band practice, since I needed to sneak off to downtown.

"Is it for a plan to kill Cassie or something?"

"No, Aiden!" I said, gasping. "Don't say things like that! An evil spirit could latch on to you when you put out that kind of bad energy!"

"Sorry, sorry, I take it back," he said. "But is it?"

"No, it's not," I said, launching into my plan to find another gifted person to help me get to wherever the Sheet Man resided.

"Wow," he said, shaking his head. "If I don't hear from you by ten tonight, I'm going to assume your soul is lost forever in some other dimension, and no, I'm not going to be the one to tell your mom."

Entering the city center of Keene was like traveling into the eighteenth century. Tall trees lined every road, and the buildings were mostly original brick construction occupied by small businesses that sported signs like YE GOODIE SHOPPE or WALPOLE CREAMERY ICE CREAM PARLOUR. A couple of church steeples soared into the sky, the only things in the city taller than the tree line.

I locked my bike up at Central Square and tuned in the spirits I'd been desperately attempting to block out during my ride so I wouldn't crash. I immediately spotted some Plegians casually hanging around the giant structure that held up all the jack-o'-lanterns during the annual pumpkin festival, comfortably reclining on it. Plegians are at once the most innocuous and the most terrifyingly destructive of demons: They don't latch onto people the way other kinds do, but they still cause needless harm. Whenever a freak accident happens—a building collapses, a car's brakes stop working, a sinkhole swallows a house—the Plegians are usually at play.

I veered far away from the structure, in case they decided to send it toppling down on me, and headed to the first address, just behind the square on Winter Street, less than two minutes away.

Downtown was looking very pleasant this time of year. The tree branches were grasping to the last stubborn, colorful leaves, and the occasional crisp breeze would sail through and wrest the leaves from the trees' grip, sending them tumbling through the air, spinning and spiraling in all directions. Lights were already strung around some of the trees, and it made the whole square look charming and welcoming.

I turned onto Winter Street and stopped dead in my tracks, inching back to hide behind the corner. Someone was exiting the tarot card shop, followed closely by a winged creature called a Bruton.

I'd seen that kind of demon only a couple of times before, but its image was seared into my brain. The face of a Bruton isn't well defined; when it moves, it blurs, so you're never sure exactly where it is or what it looks like. The wings seem too barbaric and jagged to actually fly, but they can expand as wide as a house and are extremely powerful. But the worst part, as usual, is the eyes—they're made of fire, and not the good kind of fire that I flock to, but the menacing kind that burns down houses and destroys forests.

Brutons latch onto people like other demons do, but in a more sinister way. Instead of sucking away a person's energy, they use their own negative energy to manipulate and deceive. People occasionally tell me that they have nightmares featuring scary creatures with flames for eyes and batlike wings, and I immediately hand them a candle, tell them to close their mind to negative energy, and then run far away from them. If a Bruton is passing through your dreams, you're in trouble.

The human and the demon didn't seem to notice me as they walked away, and I stayed hidden behind the corner until they were out of sight. I debated whether I should even enter the shop. If it was where Brutons regularly hung out, I didn't want to mix with that energy. But after I decided it'd be highly unlikely to have two Brutons in a small tarot card shop, I sucked up my courage and walked toward the door.

When I entered, annoying wind chimes sounded from above. "Oh, did you forget something, Miss Ti—" The clerk looked up from papers on the counter and realized I wasn't the customer who'd just left. "I'm sorry. How can I help you?"

He was a guy, probably in his early thirties, with

limbs as thin as ski poles. He'd been shuffling papers together, and I was amazed he had the strength to lift even a few pieces of them.

"Who was just in here?"

"I'm afraid my customer information is confidential."

"Well, whoever it was is in grave danger." I studied the object hanging around his neck: a pentagram, the symbol of a Wiccan.

"I see," he said curtly. "Can I help you with something?"

I hadn't asked Tommy what I should be on the lookout for. I assumed I'd know it when I saw it. "I'm not a hundred percent sure. Do you have anything that deals with, uh, other spiritual dimensions?"

"You're interested in the occult?" His eyebrows shot up. "Reaching another realm besides the physical one?"

"Sure," I said, feeling certain that if we were to nail down the specifics on what exactly he meant by that, we'd have very different opinions.

"You're just a kid," he said, rummaging around on his desk, "so I'm not going to get too into it with you, but I'd feel comfortable giving you this, at least."

He handed me a pamphlet with the words "Introduction to the Far Shadow" boldly printed on the cover.

"What's the Far Shadow?"

"Everything," he said, smiling, "and nothing."

I flipped through some of the pages. Astral dimensions. Zodiac signs. Pentagrams. Moon cycles. Ritual introductions. This wasn't going to help me find the Sheet Man.

"You might be interested in page twenty-seven," he said.

I flipped to it and read the heading: "Book of Shadows." It detailed a list of rituals and spells and some specific examples.

"The Summoning of the Far Spirits?" I said. "Why would you need to summon spirits? They're all around us."

"Some would disagree with you," he said.

Well, then, *some* were idiots who knew nothing.

"It's a challenging spell, not something you'd be able to do by any means without years of training behind you."

"Oh. Well, can you do it, then?"

He chuckled, grabbed the pamphlet back, and, in a dramatic, hushed whisper, read:

"Invoked you are
To appear at my side.
Travel through the realms

And journey to my voice,
Which beckons you past the stars,
Through the dust, and into my presence."

Nothing happened.

He frowned. "Still haven't gotten that one to work yet."

"Have you gotten *any* of them to work yet?"

"It's harder than it looks, kid." He sounded insulted. "You try it."

I sighed, knowing full well this was a huge waste of my time, but part of me felt bad I'd wounded his pride. I picked up the pamphlet, smiling earnestly at him, and recited the words.

"Invoked you are
To appear at my side.
Travel through the realms
And journey to my voice . . ."

I'd looked up to make a face that said, *You're right, this is stupidly hard*, and in that moment I learned two semirelated things. The first was that this guy was very much a fraud, in possession of no spiritual gifts whatsoever. The second was that I was very much not a fraud, because when I'd looked up, I'd seen a pair of shimmering red eyes, detached from their owner, hovering just above the skinny Wiccan guy.

I dropped the pamphlet as the eyes pierced my own with their gaze. They squinted at me curiously, as though I were some kind of circus freak.

"What's wrong, kid?" the guy asked.

"Look up," I whispered.

He looked right up at the eyes, which looked down at him in an almost pleasant way, and then he turned back to me. "What?"

"I need to leave," I said, hoping the eyes wouldn't follow me out of the store. I actually wanted to look to see if there was an opposite spell—the Unsummoning of the Far Spirits, some kind of Get the Heck Out of Here chant—but I was too afraid to touch the pamphlet again, let alone say any more of the spell, in case the rest of red-eyed entity appeared. Instead I pulled out my lighter, surrounded myself with light, and hyperblasted some positive energy at the big red eyes floating above. They squinted, more annoyed than angry, as if the flames of fire were nothing more than irritating gnats.

"Aw, come on, kid, it's only a dumb spell," the guy said, laughing. "A bunch of hocus-pocus from a dying branch of Wiccan beliefs."

I shook my head. "You need to be more careful

with that stuff." And I walked out the door.

What had just happened? Whatever it was, it didn't feel too menacing . . . it just *looked* menacing, which was almost as bad. I lit my lighter one more time for some reassurance, to make sure nothing negative had attached itself to me. I was fairly certain demons couldn't do anything to me, since Kristina's protections didn't go away simply because she did. At least, I hoped they didn't. I had no real frame of reference to work with.

I debated whether I wanted to continue after having invoked the eyes of a Far Spirit, a phrase I wanted to extinguish from my mind as soon as possible. I thought back to the creation of my talisman, the weird phrases I'd had to recite and the strange ribbons of energy. Wasn't that basically a form of pseudomagic? What else was I capable of? Shaken, but determined I was doing the right thing, I decided to keep going.

The other shop, Madame Nadirah's, was on the other side of the square, past the pumpkin-holding structure and down the main road a little bit. I admired the square again, steering clear of the Plegians and doing my best to ignore the ghosts making requests.

"Please tell my daughter she doesn't need to worry about maintaining my coin collection. I only collected them in the first place because I was so bored all the time, and I don't want her ending up the same way."

"My son's been asking for a sign from me. Go up to him and mention the explosion in Montana, he'll get a kick out of it."

"My sister is right there and needs to know her son has been experimenting with some disgusting substances. Don't walk away from me, young man. I know you can hear me."

"I'm on a mission," I hissed to them. "I don't have time to deliver your messages."

A blinking mom and her daughter looked back at me with concern, and I laughed and waved them off, which I realized only served to reaffirm that I was crazy.

By the time I reached Madame Nadirah's, I must have ignored at least ten ghosts, feeling a pit of guilt grow in my stomach with every rejection, but the good thing was that there were no Brutons or any other sort of demon lingering around the shop. It seemed nice enough. There were no tacky neon signs advertising psychic readings, nor were than any crystal balls or tarot cards in sight. There was just a sign that read MADAME NADIRAH'S MYSTIC SHOPPE, and purple curtains blocked the view inside.

I opened the door, causing a loud bell to ring from somewhere in the back. Crossing the threshold, I was sort of charmed by what I saw. There was a spinning display of books and pamphlets advertising various ways to deepen spiritual connections (DON'T HATE. MEDITATE!); a colorful selection of meditation mats lining one of the walls (A STRONG MIND MAKES A LIFE DEFINED!); posters and plaques inscribed with uplifting platitudes (CUSTOM-MADE TO FIT YOUR SPIRITUAL NEEDS!); and a massive display filled with all kinds of candles (FIND THE SCENT AND HUE THAT'S JUST RIGHT FOR YOU!).

As I was looking at a twenty-dollar candle that had sage-infused wax (BURN THE SAGE TO CLEANSE AND PURGE UNWANTED VISITORS ON THE VERGE!), a short woman with an out-of-control Afro emerged from the back room. She wore a loose-fitting green dress featuring elaborate gold stitching down the sides, and a pair of thick glasses magnified her eyes, making her pupils look twice their normal size.

"I am Madame Nadirah," she said in a breathy, excited voice. "Welcome to my shop. I notice you're looking at the spirit-cleansing candle. Are you experiencing problems in your house?"

"Uh, well, you could say that," I said, shrugging. "I'm actually not here to buy any products. I'm wondering if I could make use of your abilities."

Her eyes lit up. "Ah, you seek guidance from the

spiritual world, do you? I can help you, my child."
She stepped forward, looking me up and down and
clucking her tongue. "You seem tense. Very tense.
There is clearly something bothering you, child."

"You're off to a good start," I said, wondering
why anyone would show up to a shop like this unless
something was bothering them.

"Come, follow me, we'll sort it out together."

She headed for the back door, and we entered a
dark room lit up by black lights, causing everything
white to glow neon blue.

"Oh man." I blinked several times, hoping to make
my eyes adjust to the sudden change in light. "Wasn't
expecting that."

"I feel it's best to channel spirits in a way that can
allow their energy to radiate in a different form, one
that you may even be able to see."

"Right," I said, rolling my eyes. Kristina had told
me repeatedly that most living people couldn't see
ghosts, no matter what they claimed.

"Now, get comfortable," she said, pointing to a
glowing cushion on the floor. I took my seat across
from her, a low table between us. She had her hands
on the table, palms down, fingers spread wide apart.
A soothing song featuring low chants played quietly
from somewhere in the room, and I felt a tingle around

the base of my neck as the energy riled up around me. This woman had some kind of gift. I wasn't sure to what extent, though.

"Tell me your name, child," she said peacefully, like she was starting a mediation.

"Baylor Bosco."

"Now, Baylor, why don't you . . ."

She stopped suddenly, her illuminated eyes flicking up toward my face and zooming all over. She reached up and hit something on the wall.

The black lights went off, and a harsh fluorescent light filled the small room instead. Madame Nadirah's face had transformed from serene to irate.

"Baylor Bosco?" she spit. "Are you kidding me?" Her voice had changed as well. The breathiness had disappeared, replaced by a sharp, sassy tone. "What are you doing in my shop?"

"You've heard of me?"

"Of course I've heard of you! You're only my biggest customer stealer in the state. My shop's been open for fifteen years, and ever since you started delivering messages left and right, my business has gone down by fifty percent."

"I'm sorry," I said. "I had no idea." My hands were sweating.

"You should be sorry," she said. "It's great you've

actually been blessed with a gift and all, but a girl's gotta eat. I'm gonna have to downsize soon, you know, and the real question is how can I downsize from something that's already as tiny as a closet?"

"Wait, what do you mean that I've 'actually been blessed'? Are you saying you're—"

"Not like you," she said. "Mmm, nope. I just give good advice. This is way more fun than having to use my psychology degree."

"Are you really admitting to me you're a fraud?" I asked. "You really sit here and let people pay you for tricking them into thinking you can communicate with their loved ones?"

"I wouldn't go that far," she said. "My gift is more . . . intuitive. I could feel from the second you walked in that there was something different about you, but once you said your name, I wasn't going to sit here and let you embarrass me."

"So you've got intuition," I said. "An empath, right? I could feel that. I could feel the tingle in my neck when you were speaking. That's real, at least."

She raised her eyebrows and let out a laugh after a few seconds. "You playing?"

"No," I said. "I could feel it."

"From the horse's mouth!" she laughed, clapping her hands together. "My auntie was right. She's obsessed with you, by the way, one of those Bay-lievers. Psh. Before you were born, though, she was always saying I was special, that I knew too much. I always just thought I was a good actress."

I thought of that tingle in my neck and wondered if it had maybe been a regular itch. I blocked out that thought. She was the only person in town who could help me. "I need your help, Madame Nadirah."

Madame Nadirah did not like anything I had to say. She didn't like the Sheet Man, she didn't like know-ing my dead twin followed me around, she didn't like hearing that the dead twin had been ghostnapped, and she really, really didn't like knowing that demons were actively floating around the city.

"Those things aren't standing outside my shop, right?"

"No, and that's another reason why I trust you—they wouldn't try to influence a gifted person who had so much positive energy. It wouldn't work. That's why they leave you alone and stick to the frauds."

"Baylor, I just told you fifteen minutes ago I'm a fraud."

"You say that, but you're wrong. You've managed to keep this store open this long." I looked around the room. "You couldn't have done that if there weren't *something* here. I know you're my best bet for entering the dimension where the Sheet Man resides. If you can't help me, no one in this city can. Well, except for my baby sister, Ella, but she can't speak English yet, so for now you're it."

She sighed, twirling a curl around one of her fingers. "Fine," she said. "Fine, I'll help, but if something goes wrong, if one of those little demons swoops in and gobbles you up, don't say I didn't warn you."

"I'm not worried," I said excitedly. I reached into my backpack and pulled out the talisman. "I'm taking this with me."

"What could that be? Looks like a blind carpenter's last try."

"It's a talisman I made to stop the Sheet Man," I said.

"You make talismans?" she asked, nonplussed.

"Not regularly," I said. "This was my first time."

"Oh, Lord." She shook her head, still looking dubiously at the talisman. "Baylor, neither one of us knows what we're doing here. Even if that *thing* can protect you, how do you plan on getting to the dimension where the Sheet Man resides? Do you have a map you forgot to mention?"

I didn't want to admit I wasn't sure about that, either. I had an idea, though. I once asked Aiden what he saw when he shut his eyes, and he said everything was black, but sometimes weird purple and green squiggles and shapes would dance around aimlessly.

But for me, when I close my eyes, I initially see black, and then it's almost as if I mentally walk forward a few feet, and the black dissolves away, letting me see exactly where I am in its pure state, with flowing energies and auras and unfiltered spirits. I assumed if I focused my energy on the Sheet Man and Kristina's energies, I'd be led the right way.

"I just have a feeling," I said, hoping I sounded more confident than I felt.

We spent a few minutes going over the basics and coming up with the necessary protections. Then we got started.

"Lie down, child," she said, her voice losing its edge and taking on that breathy quality. "Get comfortable."

I sprawled out on the floor of the tiny back room and placed my head on the cushion. She flipped the black lights back on.

"Really?"

"Hey, you said I had intuition, and this is where I

feel it the strongest. If you can have a talisman with an egg, I can have a room with some black lights."

"Fine." I shut my eyes.

She placed four sage candles around me, two by my wrists and two by my ankles. As she lit each one, she recited the phrase we came up with: "Let the fire shackle this body to the earth. Let my spirit keep him safe."

With each candle I imagined a fiery handcuff shooting out from the wick and wrapping itself around my wrist or ankle. This ritual was to make sure I wouldn't be trapped in some other dimension while my body lay vulnerable in Madame Nadirah's shop. Otherwise, I'd be easy prey for an insidious, sneaky Insymbio to take over my being.

Once she was done lighting the candles, she placed her hands over my fast-beating heart and recited another phrase: "Let his soul find the path to healing. Let his light expel the darkness."

I felt secure and at peace knowing my body was protected and Madame Nadirah was keeping watch. I let my mind calm down and thought of nothing but Kristina and the Sheet Man.

Kristina, if you're there, if you can hear me, if you can feel me, then lead the way.

It felt daunting. Although I was lying still and

motionless, I was overwhelmed by how tired I suddenly felt. Kristina was so far away. How would I be able to find her?

But slowly the black faded away, and the room materialized back into view. It was quieter, grayer. Madame Nadirah had disappeared, and I could feel an energy lifting my spirit. The feeling of exhaustion had vanished. I pushed myself up and cautiously stepped out of my body and into another dimension, hoping I wasn't making a terrible mistake.

I walked outside the shop, talisman in hand, and saw no one. The only things in this particular dimension were most likely me, the Sheet Man, and Kristina.

Strange shadows floated by me, and I wondered if they were shadows of spirits, somehow reflected into this new dimension. The only question now was where to find the Sheet Man. I felt like there was a good chance that he would come to me if I was exposed for long enough.

I walked up the main road, back to Central Square, and saw the massive structure where the demons had been reclining. The demons were gone, but two large shadows were in their place. I kept my distance. I didn't know if I had any protections from them in this dimension, and I didn't want to test it.

I walked the square once, then headed down the deserted road in the direction where I lived. There was a chance he could be at my house, but it was a real shot in the dark.

"Sheet Man!" I called out. "Kristina!"

Nothing.

Everything around me looked duller and life-less. It was almost like the city I'd grown up in, but through some bizarre, groggy filter; the spark that made it colorful and lively was gone. It seemed like joy couldn't possibly exist here, like a permanent winter.

"Sheet Man! Alfred! Alfred Parker!" I called out. I had nothing to lose, right? Since I was the only one making noise in this dimension, I figured the sound would carry to wherever he was.

"Kristina!"

A fierce wind picked up, howling in my ears. I looked around, wondering which direction I could expect to see him coming from, when an odd flicker appeared in front of me, as though this dimension offered poor reception.

After several flickers, in and out, Grandpa Bosco burst through in a shower of blue sparks, his body outlined in blue light.

I hadn't seen him since he disappeared with

Kristina to the Beyond more than five years ago, and boy, did he look pissed off to see me.

"What in the Almighty are you doing here, Baylor?" he growled over the wind, grabbing my arm. It was the strangest feeling, like I'd gotten the chills but only in the area of my arm where he was holding on to me.

"Grandpa! What are you doing?"

"Getting you out of here!" He was dragging me back in the direction of the square, his thin hair whipping around in the intensifying wind. "That Tommy told you to come here, didn't he? Darn it, Baylor, just because we're ghosts doesn't mean you can always assume we're right."

"But, Grandpa, Kristina is trapped in here somewhere," I said, trying to pry his hand off my arm, but I couldn't penetrate the blue energy surrounding his body.

"I know that, you dimwit," he said. "But she's dead. She can be here and not be harmed. You, on the other hand, are very much alive, and if something happens to you, you could be stuck in this limbo forever."

"I've got the talisman, Grandpa, I'll be fine."

"Do you think the Sheet Man is the only entity in this dimension?" he said, his eyes wide and grave. "You've got one talisman, but what if another demon attacks you after you've already used it? You can't imagine the kinds of creatures that have been banished to this dimension." His grip tightened as the blue light seemed to intensify. "Bam. You'd be done, Baylor, with no chance of ever entering the Beyond, and frankly, we can't have that."

"If I don't do this, I might never see Kristina again!" I was banging the wooden bowl against his hand, but he didn't seem to notice.

"You'll see her again," he said. "You will. I wouldn't let my granddaughter languish over here otherwise. But it's part of her journey, not yours."

"What? Really?"

"Really," he said. We were nearly back in front of Madame Nadirah's by now. "Baylor, don't you ever come to this dimension again, do you understand me? It takes an enormous amount of energy for a spirit like me to cross that barrier, and I won't be able to rescue you again. Not for a few years at least."

"Okay," I said, only just realizing I was crying. "I'm sorry. I won't. It . . . it was good seeing you, Grandpa. I hope you're doing okay in the Beyond."

His eyes lightened for a moment. "I don't mean to sound so harsh, Baylor. It's a treat to see you, you've gotten so tall!" He half smiled. "I just need to make sure you're safe. I'm learning a lot, buddy boy. I hope to be able to visit you soon."

I could feel his grip loosening, but I didn't want him to let go.

"One more thing, Baylor: Tell your dad to stop worrying. He made the right choice."

Before I could ask what he meant, he tossed me through the door of the shop, and I zoomed back to my body in fast-forward motion, the shop blurring around me as I soared past the books and candles, into the room with the black lights, and onto the cushion, where I suddenly gasped and rocketed up.

Madame Nadirah was standing over me, her palms still over my heart.

"There you are," she said. "You'd gone away for a little while."

I looked around, trying to breathe and swallow at the same time, but instead choking on phlegm.

"Did it work?"

"No," I said, my body shaking and my arm still tingling from where my grandpa had had his iron grip. "Well, yes, it worked, but I didn't do what I wanted to do. My grandpa entered the dimension, yelled at me for being there, and brought me back here. I didn't want to come back yet, but he told me I could get trapped over there forever."

She was massaging my shoulders now and clucking her tongue.

"Child, if there's one thing I know in this life, it's this: When your granddaddy tells you to run, you run."

19

Clarinets can double as weapons.

AFTER ONE LONG, DAZED BIKE RIDE HOME I sneaked past the family room, where I could hear everyone hanging out, and called Aiden from my room.

"I saw my grandpa," I said. "The first time in five years."

"That's pretty cool."

"Yeah."

"So did you find Kristina?"

"No."

"Oh," he said. A silent moment passed. "J texted me while you were doing your stuff."

"What did she say?"

"She asked if she could borrow my speech notes tomorrow, she thinks she might have missed something."

I blinked. "That's all she said? I thought you were going to tell me something good about the dance."

"Oh. No."

"It's been two days," I said. "You need to figure something out."

"I'm no good at this stuff, Baylor," he said. "You've got to help me out, man."

"How? Tell me what to do, and I'll do it."

"Ask Cassie out. You're better looking than me."

"Tell me to do anything else, and I'll do it."

"Baylor, dude, come on!" he pleaded. "You've got to do this for me."

I sighed. "Cassie isn't my type. I know she looks innocent, but I have it on good authority she's into some pretty messed-up stuff."

"What? Why didn't you mention this before?"

"It's my burden to know this kind of stuff about girls. It's not fair for me to spoil your life adventures, Aiden."

"It is if she's a devil worshipper or something!" he whispered, petrified.

"It's not that bad."

"Well, it's only going to get worse in my head if you don't tell me anything else."

"One word: taxidermy."

"Oh my . . ."

I'd heard from one of her dead uncles that she was quite good at it too, a skill she'd learned from her family's annual hunting trips.

"I don't do hunting and dead stuffed animals, but that doesn't mean you can't grow to like them."

"I don't want to grow to like anything about Cassie," he said. "The only thing I want to grow to like is J, and I don't even have any more growing to do. I love her, dude."

He sounded so pained, like his heart was being sawed slowly in half.

"We'll think of something," I said. "Don't worry about it."

I wanted to tell Aiden that his problem with J and Cassie was rearing its head at a terribly inconvenient time, and if he could just put everything on hold for a few days, that'd be great. But friends don't do that, so I held my breath and tried to pretend that his problems were as important as mine.

After I hung up with Aiden, I headed downstairs to find my dad. I needed to tell him that I saw Grandpa today, but I was worried he'd react in the same way as when he witnessed my interaction with Aunt Hilda and Marjorie.

I found him playing with Ella on the floor of the family room, which simply meant they were smacking some dolls around, while Jack played a video game. My mom was snuggled up on the couch reading one of her romance novels with a shirtless guy on the cover, a glass of red wine in hand.

I watched the four of them for a minute, thinking about Kristina and feeling lucky I got to be an active part of this family, even if I was permanently grounded. I couldn't imagine always watching from the sidelines.

"Hey, buddy," my dad called to me, his voice giddy. Clearly he was in la-la land with a one-year-old. "Want to show Ella how ladies should be treated?" He reached out for a Barbie and held it next Mr. Potato Head. "With respect and courtesy," he said in a weird, vaguely Irish accent. "Don't put up with anyone who doesn't treat you like the wonderful person you are."

"Dad, I think you're getting to that point of playing with Ella where terrible ideas seem like good ones," I said.

He laughed. "You could be right." He examined my face, pushed himself onto his elbows, and frowned. "You look weird, Baylor. What's up?"

I saw my mom tense ever so slightly on the couch, and I knew she wouldn't flip another page until I was done speaking.

"I have something to tell you," I said slowly, sitting on the ground next to him. "But I need you to brace yourself for it."

My mom's grip on her book tightened until it looked like she was accosting the shirtless guy, and my dad tried to make his face as expressionless as possible.

"What is it, son?" he asked, his voice slightly deeper than normal. For a fleeting second I was sort of amused thinking of all the things they were bracing for me to tell them. How much more trouble could I really get into?

"Okay," I said, drawing it out. "Here goes."

My mom, her entire body clenched, looked like she was about to explode.

"I saw Grandpa Bosco today."

For a moment there was total silence. Even Jack's video game quieted down. Then the reaction from both my parents was instantaneous.

My mom threw her book down and—wineglass still in hand—ran to the kitchen, grabbed an old rutabaga she'd purchased by accident at the farmer's market, and began hacking at it with her chef's knife.

My dad, in that same moment, dropped both Mr. Potato Head and Barbie, grabbed a blanket from the couch, and, my fears coming true, wrapped himself up like a frightened woodland creature.

Jack and I met eyes, and his eyebrows shot up before he returned to his game. Over the rutabaga mutilation occurring in the kitchen—*clang, clang, clang!*—I said, "Dad? Are you all right?"

"Just fine," he said, his voice muffled through the blanket. "Really! I'm *fine.*"

"Okay," I said casually, acting along. "Great. So, yeah, I saw your dad, and it only lasted a couple of minutes because, well, it's a long, weird ghost story that you'd really hate, but he looked good." I paused, but he didn't say anything. "He said he's been learning a lot in the Beyond, and that he's going to try to come visit soon."

The chopping grew louder.

"There's one other thing. . . ."

He poked his head out of the blanket and stared up at me like some sort of sad turtle. "What?"

"He said to stop worrying. You made the right choice."

His eyes widened slightly, then he nodded and returned to his hole.

"What does that mean?" I asked.

"I'm just going to stay in here for a little bit."

"Okay," I said, standing back up. "Well, if you want to talk about it any more, I'll be upstairs."

"Uh-huh," he said, sounding just like a five-year-old. I mouthed "Good luck" to Jack before heading to the stairs. As I passed my mom in the kitchen, she whispered, "Baylor!" I turned to see the most finely minced vegetable I'd ever seen sitting in a light-yellow pile on her cutting board. There were even some little pieces stuck in her hair. "What on earth do I do with a rutabaga?"

At school the next morning J took me aside wordlessly, pushed me up against a locker, and crossed her arms.

"What is taking so long, Baylor? I need an answer today."

"I, uh, I . . . you see, a problem arose, J," I said, trying to choose my words carefully. I didn't want to sell out Aiden, but then it occurred to me that it might be the perfect thing to do.

"What sort of problem?"

"Aiden is so bad at life that he accidentally asked Clarinet Cassie to the dance," I said breathlessly, "and now he doesn't know how to break off their date so he can go with you instead."

"Oh," she said, taking a step back and adjusting

her bright-pink glasses. "Okay. Well, maybe I can take care of that."

"Wait, what?" I asked. "What are you going to do?"

She walked away without answering, the brain beneath her bouncing hair obviously filling with ideas, and I wondered if I'd made a huge mistake.

Just before my lunch period I heard whispers from people, and I thought I heard the name Cassie mentioned a couple of times, and it was pretty distinct, because Cassie never gets talked about.

I furrowed my eyebrows, but I didn't ask questions because, frankly, I hoped I'd imagined it.

Sitting down at my normal spot, I took a second to check my phone and saw a text message from Reverend Henry asking me to stop by after school. He almost never texted me, so I was anxious to find out what he wanted, but that thought left my mind as soon as a pair of gruff hands clamped my shoulders and pushed me hard.

"What did you do, Baylor?"

Aiden's face was bright red as he hovered behind me, dropping his backpack to the ground.

"What are you talking about?"

"Haven't you heard? Everyone else has."

I shook my head.

"Apparently, J went up to Cassie between second and third periods and asked if it would be okay if she went with me to the dance," he said, his arms flailing like a madman while he glared at me. "But Cassie said it wouldn't be okay and told J that *she* had a massive crush on me, and no one was going to stop us from going together, which caused J to say that Cassie was being unreasonable, since I'm better friends with J, and that Cassie was just being self-ish, which caused Cassie to slap J in the face *with her clarinet* and tackle her to the ground."

I looked to the side of him but saw nothing. Kristina's absence was all too glaring in this moment. Not only would she have already informed me about the girls' tussle, but she would also have reacted perfectly to Aiden's dramatic telling of it.

"That's insane," I said. "But why are you mad at me?"

"Because you told J about Cassie," he said.

"But I told you about J in the first place."

"So? You're supposed to tell me that because we're bros. But you can't go back to the original girl and tell her about the second girl that I never told the original girl about."

I put a hand up. "This is getting confusing."

"You talked to J when you should have kept your mouth shut!"

"No, she talked to me and said that she needed an answer by today, and since you said you had no idea what to do last night, I seized the opportunity, Aiden. I seized it hard, and apparently J seized some opportunities, and now it looks like all the seizing going on today has failed miserably."

"I'm pissed at you," he said, finally sitting. "None of this would have ever happened if you hadn't said anything. Now Cassie's probably getting suspended, and J's gonna have a bruise on her face in the shape of Cassie's clarinet."

"You're looking at this all wrong," I said, shaking my head in disbelief. "Aiden, two girls were fighting over you today. When has that ever happened to you? When will it ever happen again? You should go find J right now, thank her for fighting over you and getting everyone talking about you, and then kiss her."

His mouth hung open a bit, and he blinked rapidly.

"Oh my God," he said. "You're right."

"I know I'm right."

"I've got to find J."

"You've got to find her right now."

And, leaving his belongings behind, he stood up and half ran, half waddled inside to wherever J was.

* * *

I didn't hear anything about Aiden or J for the rest of the day, and once school ended, the thought of their troubles left my mind, usurped by the curiosity of what Reverend Henry had for me. It wasn't that far of a walk from school, and by the time I got to the church, I had decided that the reason he'd asked me to come by was that Kristina had visited him in a dream and told him of some way to find her.

The reverend was in his office doing paperwork when I knocked. He peered up for a moment, smiled, and said, "Just a second." He was writing furiously onto a sheet of paper and finished by flourishing his signature dramatically.

"I have something for you, Baylor," he said excitedly, reaching into his pocket for a crinkled ball of paper and handing it to me.

"Oh," I said, taking it. "Trash. Thanks."

"Open it up."

It took me a second to wrangle it open, and I smoothed the paper against the edge of his desk. An address—8736 Triumph Lane, Brattleboro, Vermont—was scrawled across the page in crude handwriting.

I glanced from the paper to Reverend Henry's toothy grin. "What is this?"

"We found it in a pocket of a pair of the pants donated by the same person who donated the shoes," he said. "I looked it up online, and it's a nursing home! That explains why 'A. Parker' was written on the shoes."

"A nursing home? That doesn't make sense. I spoke with Alfred's daughter, and she told me his new wife took care of him at home."

Reverend Henry raised an eyebrow. "I say we go find out."

"Mom, I'm spending some time with Reverend Henry this afternoon," I said on the phone a few minutes later as we sailed down the highway.

"Oh, that's great," she said brightly. "I think that's just what you need after the last few days. Tell him I said hi."

"Will do!"

"Are you going to be back in time for dinner?"

"Um, I think so," I said. "Just put any leftovers in the fridge."

"You *think* so?" she said, her voice suddenly edgy. "What are you doing that's going to take so long?"

"Okay, got to go, love you!" I hung up. "Mom says hi."

"Oh, that's wonderful," he said lightly. "I would tell her hi back, but your suspiciously abrupt end to the conversation has rendered that all but impossible."

For the thirty-minute ride I filled him in on the events from the day before, which he listened to in pursed-lip silence.

"I can't believe you would do something so reckless, Baylor," he said once I'd finished, sounding genuinely mad. "I'm glad your grandpa was there to slap some sense back into you."

"I was just trying to do a good thing," I said defensively.

"And cause irreparable damage to your soul in the process."

"You and my grandpa should get together and start a Pessimism Club."

"That's a great idea," he said. "For our first meeting we can talk about how this irresponsible kid we know has made us *pessimistic* about the intelligence of modern youths, since he goes off alone into other spiritual realms with no real protection or plan."

"Well, that doesn't sound like a fun club at all."

"It's a club for pessimists, Baylor. It's not supposed to be fun."

We pulled up in front of a stately brick building adorned with white shutters and white trim and white window boxes. The sign on the fence guarding the property read WHITE FIELDS RETIREMENT HOME.

It wasn't nearly as bad as I'd pictured. I had expected dead weeds everywhere and doors hanging off hinges, and I was surprised to see it actually looked pretty nice. The movies had warped my image of nursing homes.

Inside the lobby a teenage girl manned the reception desk, while several elderly people slowly milled about. I was desperately tuning out the huge throng of ghosts knocking to get through to me; this was no time to deliver messages. Instead I made a mental note to hold a healing session here soon.

"Hello!" said the girl at the front desk. Her name tag read ASHLEE.

"Hi, Ashlee," I said. "I was wondering if you could provide some information about a resident for me."

"I'm sorry, I can't give out resident information unless the resident is accompanying you."

"Right, well, that's sort of impossible, since the resident I'm looking for is dead."

"Oh," she said. "Well, information about any current or past resident is still confidential. I'm sorry."

She frowned like she meant it.

"Excuse me, miss," Reverend Henry said, brushing past me. "I'm sorry to cut off your conversation, but the father of one of my worshippers is near death, and I need to find his room as fast as possible."

"Oh my," she said. "Who is the resident?"

"Ken DeWong," he said. "Please hurry."

Ashlee typed something into her computer, and seconds later she said, "He's in room seventeen G. You're going to need to walk down the hall, turn left, and then go through the door on the right, which will lead you to the G wing of the—"

"I'm much too upset to remember any of what you're saying," he said, talking at an impossibly fast pace. "Can you just lead me there?"

"I'm not supposed to leave my desk unattended, though," she said, eyeing me nervously. "I can call someone to take you there."

"I was just on the phone with Ken's son, and he told me every second counted," Reverend Henry said so earnestly that I almost grabbed his arm to lead him to the room myself. "Please."

She studied his face and sighed. "Okay," she said, getting up. "Follow me." She looked at me and said, "I'm sorry, I'll be right back if you don't mind waiting for a moment."

She touched Reverend Henry's back and guided him forward, and he glanced back to give me a quick but pointed look. Once they turned the corner, I circled around the desk, took her seat, and examined the database she had open on the screen.

In the search bar on the top right she had typed "DeWong," so I deleted it and typed "Parker." I got six results back, and sure enough, one of them was "Parker, Alfred."

I clicked on the name, and the first thing that popped up was all his basic information. I grabbed the notepad on her desk and began scrawling the information as fast as I could. I wasn't sure how much time I had, so I didn't bother looking down, hoping that it would all be legible later.

"Angela Mendoza-Parker," I muttered to myself as I copied the emergency contact information. "There's your phone number. Let's hope it didn't change."

I finished writing, searched for "DeWong" again, and then circled back around the desk and out of the door before Ashlee reappeared.

I ran to the parking lot and found Reverend Henry already in the car.

"How did you beat me here?"

"Ashlee took me to the room, and I told her to leave before I went in, since it was such a somber moment, and when she turned the corner, I walked out of the emergency exit and came right back here."

"Sly move coming up with that story, Reverend," I said. "I didn't know you had it in you."

"Mr. DeWong's son owed me one, so it's all right," he said.

"Well, I got a phone number, among other information," I said.

"Call it!"

"And say what? 'I know you're causing your dead husband to attack me, you gold digger!'?"

"Here, give that to me," he said, taking the paper and pulling out his cell phone. He typed in the numbers and held the phone to his ear.

"Yes, hi, I'm looking for Angela? . . . Oh, this is she, good. Well, Angela, you made a donation to Keene Community Church recently, and we found an item of value in one of the pockets and figured that you might want it back, since it probably wasn't intended as a donation."

My jaw nearly fell into my lap as I watched him lie so effortlessly.

"Oh, what item is it? I'm afraid I'm not permitted to say over the phone; it's something I can discuss only in person, unfortunately. . . . Yes, you're definitely going to want it. I may be a reverend, but I know an expensive thing when I see it." He laughed heartily. "Tomorrow would be ideal, yes. . . . Noon? Is that the only time you're available?"

I shook my head vigorously. I couldn't miss school again.

"Ah, you're traveling tomorrow night. Got it. Okay, well, noon works. Just come inside the church and look for the office that says 'Reverend Henry.' Okay, thanks, Angela. . . . Oh, it's *Ahn*-hell-uh? Great, thanks for letting me know. See you then."

He hung up and looked at me with the strangest expression on his face.

"I keep sinning today," he said. "It's ironic that such behavior is on behalf of the person with the most direct connection to the afterlife that I know of."

"I can't miss school again tomorrow, Reverend Henry!"

"Listen, if I can lie to two separate people in the space of ten minutes, knowing it's for a good intention, then surely you can figure out a way to get to the church tomorrow during your lunch period."

Don't cry
at school.

I HAD NEVER BEEN CHALLENGED BY A REV-
erend before, and I figured if he could bend the rules
a little bit, then so could I.

After getting dropped off at home, I debated
whether or not I should just tell my mom and ask
for a note to leave school early tomorrow, but I knew
she would say no, go on a diatribe about the curse
that was my gift, remind me that I was supposed to
be grounded for all eternity, and then call the school
tomorrow to check if I was still there.

I also knew full well that she would be equally mad if

she found out I got caught skipping. It seemed doomed to be a lose-lose situation, and since Kristina wasn't there to offer advice, I chose the side of less confrontation.

Aiden was having confrontation troubles as well. He called me that night to give me the full report on what had happened.

"I found her in the nurse's office," he said.

"And?"

"And that rat-faced, turd-lipped freak Andrew was there."

"What? Why?"

"He didn't hear *why* she'd been attacked, just that some band nerd started beating her with a clarinet."

"So what'd you do?"

"I ran!"

"Aiden!"

"I couldn't help it!" he said, distraught.

"Did she see you?"

"I don't think so. I just saw Andrew there petting her face with his scaly little hands."

"Well," I said, "that's no good."

"What should I do?"

I tried to put myself in J's shoes and imagine what she would do in that situation.

"Aiden, you need to call her right now and tell her you want to go to the dance with her."

"Isn't this sort of thing better in person?"

"Not when you have a cretin like Andrew hovering over her like an alien spaceship, ready to beam her up and away from you. Do it. Now."

Before I'd finished speaking, Aiden started fiddling with some buttons on his phone.

"Aiden?" I said.

No response, more beeps, then ringing.

"Oh no," I muttered. But I couldn't hang up. I should have, but I couldn't.

"Hello?" J said rather reluctantly.

"I love you!" Aiden blurted out. "I've loved you for a whole year and didn't have the courage to say it until today. Until you got beat up . . . for me."

My jaw hit the ground.

"You . . . you love me?"

"Uh, yes," he said, his voice nearly gone, replaced by a high-pitched squeal. "I think I do."

"I got hit in the face today, and you didn't even come see me."

"That's not true," he said. "I did visit, but Andrew was standing there, and I didn't know what to do."

"You should have knocked him out of the way, Aiden," she said, clearly exasperated. "You couldn't man up for five measly seconds?"

"I . . . I . . . that's not what I thought you'd say."

"I'm not trying to be mean," she said, more frantic than I'd ever her sound before. "I'm confused. You *love* me? But you couldn't muster up the courage to come say a simple hello after I got slapped in the face and blindsided by a clarinet for you."

"J, just say you love him back!" I yelled.

Radio silence.

"Baylor?" she said, sounding like she was trying to hold in vomit.

"You're still here?" Aiden shrieked, horrified.

"Uh," I said, panicking. "Yeah. Ha, ha. You didn't disconnect my call."

"And you didn't hang up yourself?"

"This isn't about me, okay? Let's get back to you two."

"Well, I'd *love* to continue this chat," J shouted, "but my mortification quota has been maxed out for the day, so . . . I'm going to go."

"What? No!" Aiden said. "You can't leave me hanging after I just told you . . . all those things."

"I need to process this, Aiden," she said. "I hope you understand. And good night, Baylor." Her voice sounded particularly venomous.

We heard a click, we sat for a moment in suffocating silence, and then Aiden said, "Good advice, dude."

"Sorry, Aiden," I said. "I really thought that was going to work."

"Well, it didn't."

And he hung up too.

School the next morning was somehow more uncomfortable than the phone call. Aiden wasn't talking to me, but then, he wasn't talking to anyone. He sat at his desk with his head pressed into his arms, which were forming a barricade to the outside world.

When I saw J, she tried to avoid making eye contact, but I grabbed her arm and pulled her aside.

"Listen, J, I've got a lot of things on my plate right now, and frankly, the last thing I need is any drama between you, me, and Aiden. Just tell the kid you'll go to the dance with him."

"Seriously, Baylor?" She hiked up her backpack around her shoulders and made herself a few inches taller. "This isn't even about the dance anymore. He told me he loves me. First off, that's crazy. Second, normal people in love usually act like they're, you know, in love."

"Right, J, but in case you haven't noticed, Aiden's never been too concerned with acting normal. He's shy, and an empty bucket has more self-esteem than him. Don't punish him just because he believes he's not good enough for you, okay?"

It was at this moment the tears chose to spill out

as Kristina's words from our big fight spewed out of my mouth.

"He just wants to be with you, J. He just wants to love you and hug you and kiss you, and he really means it when he says he loves you. You can't hurt him, J."

J shushed me and awkwardly smiled at all the people walking by and staring at us. "What's gotten into you, Baylor?"

"I just really miss Kr—"

But I stopped short. J didn't know about Kristina.

No one knew about Kristina except for a handful of people. It hit me how totally invisible and forgotten and extraneous she must have felt.

She didn't even have a tombstone in the cemetery as a small reminder that she was a person. She had her own personality and sense of humor and quirks, but no one knew her.

And she was the person I trusted the most out of anyone.

And she was missing in some ghost world and I might never see her again.

The tears weren't stopping, and J was on her tiptoes trying to block my face from everyone passing by.

"Baylor, who's 'Kr—'? Who were you going to say?"

I puffed out my chest and looked her right in the eye.

"Kristina. My twin. My unborn twin, who walks with me through life and helps me manage all the spirits I can communicate with."

J's frozen face told me I should have kept my mouth shut.

"Baylor, you had a twin?"

"I have a twin. Kristina's real, and Aiden is in love with you, and your grandma with crazy hoop earrings thinks you'd be a fool not to pick Aiden, and you're just going to have to deal with it."

"He's such a cutie!" her grandma squealed as she tried in vain to push J's hair back.

I turned and walked away.

"Deal with which one?" she called out, sounding genuinely confused.

"All of it!" I yelled, and a couple of girls next to me jumped in terror.

My eyes were probably still red and wet when Bobby saw me and raised his eyebrows.

"Dude, what happened to you?"

"Allergies," I sniffled. "Really bad allergies."

At quarter past eleven I sneaked out of school and felt my feet propelling me forward to the church. I was clutching the talisman with both hands and muttering about light and positivity under my breath, and to anyone unlucky enough to see me on the street, I probably looked like a ranting lunatic.

The reverend was waiting for me outside the church.

"Oh, good!" he said as I walked through the parking lot to the entrance. "You made it."

"I am so ready for this all to be over," I said.

"Well, she'll be here soon enough," he said. "Hopefully, we'll have our answers."

He eyed the talisman in my hands.

"Expecting a visit from the Sheet Man as well?"

"You never know," I said. "If Angela's the cause of all this evil, then I need to be ready."

He pulled out the cross chain that was hidden below his shirt and smiled. "I'll be ready too."

We walked inside and waited in the office.

At ten past noon Angela Mendoza-Parker strolled into the office. She was a woman in her midthirties, and though it was a Thursday afternoon, she was wearing a hot-pink dress and black heels. Her hair was a nice-looking bundle of curls.

"*Hola!*" she said. "I'm looking for Rrrreverend Henry?"

"That's me," he said, standing up and extending his arms. "Thank you for coming."

She smiled one of those smiles where she scrunched

her eyes and cheeks together, but her mouth didn't
move. "You found something espensive?" She saw me
glaring at her, and since I also happened to be holding
a primitive wooden bowl with an egg resting in it, she
immediately assumed I was insane. "Oh, I so sorry to
interrupt your time with a . . . a child of God."

"No, it's fine," Reverend Henry said. "Baylor is
actually the reason I called you here today."

She blinked, scrunching her eyes up again. "I don't
understand. I thought you found something? I was
thinking a watch or a necklez?"

Reverend Henry looked at me and raised his eyebrows. I stood up, clutching the talisman tightly, and
swallowed hard.

"Angela, my name is Baylor Bosco, and I can
communicate with people who have crossed over.
Your husband, Alfred, has been haunting me, and
now he's taken a ghost hostage in whatever limbo
he's trapped in."

Her lips, covered in bright-red lipstick, spread a
centimeter apart.

"I know who you are," she said. "You're a devil
man. I leaving."

"No!" I yelled as she turned away. "I know what
you did!" She froze and looked back, her face finally
showing some genuine emotion: fear.

"That's right," I continued, taking a step forward. "I know all about how you married Alfred for his money and then ripped off his kids, making sure they got nothing."

Her reaction was not what I expected. Rather than appearing remorseful or even acting out in rage, her face sank into relief.

"You don't know anything," she said quietly, and she turned and rushed out of the room.

"Wait!" I said, following her out the door and past some pews. "You can't just leave."

"You have no idea what you're talking about," she yelled, picking up her pace. There were a few scattered people sitting in the pews, looking over in shock.

"Then tell me what I need to know so he'll leave me alone!"

"I loved him," she said, practically running to the door. "And it's none of your business."

She had just burst through the doors when I took a running leap forward and grabbed on to her arm. My hand slid down and touched the gold bracelet she wore around her wrist, and suddenly a vision flashed through my head. I saw a hazy, dark room occupied by Angela and another woman.

"This is just the first of many gifts," the other

woman said, holding the same bracelet Angela was wearing, "if you agree to the terms, of course."

"It's not right," Angela said.

"Alfred's the devil, honey," said the other woman. "Just think of yourself as a guardian angel making things right."

Angela was frowning, but she was also hungrily eyeing the bracelet. She was dressed in baggy clothes, and her hair looked like black straw.

"He deserves what's coming to him, and we'll all be better off," the other woman said.

Angela nodded to her, her jaw clenched. "I'll do it."

And then the most wicked laughter erupted from the other woman, Rosalie, such terrible, cacophonous glee that I screwed up my eyes and pressed my hands to my ears, and suddenly the vision was gone.

"You're a liar!" I yelled as Angela came back into view in the parking lot. She had clearly just relived the same memory attached to the bracelet, because her legs shook violently and her heels seemed in danger of cracking in half. "You've got to be kidding me! You and Rosalie plotted against Alfred? She got you to marry him so that you could steal the money from his children?"

"It's not like that!" Angela said, tears streaming

down her face. "I was broke, and Rosalie found me and took me under her wing." She wiped away the tears with both hands, her eyes pleading with me. "She got me back on my feet, and then . . . she asked for a favor."

I shook my head. "You are a horrible person. No wonder Alfred's been haunting me."

"No!" she cried. "There's more to it. Once I got to know Alfred, everything changed. He was sweet to me, and he cared about me, and I took care of him."

"No you didn't," I spit. "You put him in a nursing home and told his kids he lived at home!"

"He told me to!" she said, her voice rasping. "He was getting sick in the head, and he didn't want to be a burden. He really loved me." She swallowed hard. "At least, I thought he did. The day he died, a note showed up in my room."

"What did it say?"

She reached into her purse as tears dripped down her nose and onto the pavement. She pulled out an envelope and handed it to me. "I carry it with me everywhere."

On the crinkled front of the envelope Alfred had written "Angie" in neat cursive.

I pulled out the letter, unfolded it, and scanned the page.

Angie,

We met tonight for the first time, and I plan on marrying you. Why? Because I know Rosalie put you up to this, and since I'm so old and you're so pretty, I thought, why not have some fun in my final years? I know Rosalie is after my money, and the old bag is dim enough to think she can outsmart me. My kids each have a secret trust they'll gain access to when they're 30. I want them to work hard and live normal lives until then.

As for the rest of my money, you can have it. I've learned a lot about you and know you need it. Help your family out. Do some good with it. All I ask is that you don't share it with Rosalie. That witch would run off with it all and leave our kids penniless if she had her way.

Thank you, Angie. I hope you're happy with me.

Al

I looked at Angela in disbelief. "Alfred knew?"

She nodded. "The whole time. And he never said a word."

"So did you keep his promise?"

She bit her lip and nodded. "Yes. After he died, I disappeared, and Rosalie got *nada*. I didn't even go to his funeral because I was so scared I would see her."

I stared in horror. "So if you're not the one who's cursed Alfred into some weird limbo, that means . . ."

"Rosalie." She nodded, wide eyed. "This is my first time back in town since he died, and I'm only here to clear out what's left of Alfred's things. I don't want her to know. She's into awful things that give me heebie-jeebies."

"This all makes sense," I said, a million thoughts rushing through my brain. "You're the only one who knows the truth, and you've been away for years. Alfred needed me to find you so that you could tell me and so that I could . . ." The words sputtered. What was I going to do to Rosalie? Kindly ask her to stop cursing Alfred's name? That probably wouldn't go over well.

"I have to go," I said faintly. "Thank you, Angela. I hope you're spreading the good with his money."

"I have formed a charity in Colombia," she said proudly. "Alfred's memory lives on through the bright eyes of my country's poorest children."

"Yeah, that's great," I said, turning away. "See you!"

But I didn't have to go far, since Reverend Henry was standing outside.

"Well, that was interesting," he said. "What happened with the bracelet? You touched it, and then all of a sudden you both looked shocked and you started yelling about Rosalie."

"There was a memory attached to it," I said, and I quickly explained everything I'd learned. "Can you take me to Winchester? We've got to pay Rosalie a visit."

Reverend Henry looked at me, horrified. "That's a lot to take in, Baylor." He checked his watch, hesitated, and said, "My next appointment is a lost cause anyway. Let's go."

TIP

21

Sticks and stones do more than break bones.

"SHOULD WE TELL THE POLICE WHERE we're going, Baylor?" Reverend Henry asked as we sped down the highway. "Is this woman dangerous?"

"She's only dangerous if you're already dead," I said.

My spine was tingling. I knew the Sheet Man mystery was going to be solved today, and I was excited to have Kristina back. I wondered if she would have any good stories to tell me.

"What about your parents?" he asked. "Do they know you're here?"

"Uhh, not exactly," I said breathily.

"Baylor, please do not tell me you cut school and didn't tell your parents."

"I didn't think they would enjoy hearing about this very much."

"You're going to get me in trouble," he said, shaking his head. "I'm going to be cast out of my church because of you."

"Well, hopefully, you'll be rewarded richly in the Beyond for all your efforts."

He side-eyed me and shook his head.

We pulled up outside of Rosalie's charming cottage a little while later, and I found it odd that someone so terrible could inhabit such a nice home. It was the exact same situation with humans, though—sometimes the ugliest souls lived in the best-looking people.

"You can stay here," I said to Reverend Henry. "I can take care of this on my own."

He threw his head back and laughed. "Yeah, right, Baylor," he said, unbuckling his seat belt. "Let's go."

We got out and walked up the brick path to her home. The dogs started barking before we'd even made it up the steps to her porch.

"They don't sound very friendly," the reverend said.

I knocked, but no one answered.

"Doesn't look like she's home," he said.

I knocked once more, and this time the door opened just as my fist collided with it.

I looked over at the reverend, but he was gone. In fact, most of the color from the street was gone. The back of my neck tingled. *This is it.* The talisman was shaking in my hands. I only wished I could blame it on some kind of supernatural power instead of my nerves.

I crossed through the threshold and found myself in a narrow foyer. I could go either left or straight. Something told me to go left.

I turned the corner, and standing in the sparsely decorated living room was Rosalie, dressed in red sweatpants and a tight white shirt. She held in her hand a length of white material, the same as what covered the Sheet Man, who was standing right next to her with the other end of the material around his neck, like a dog on a leash.

My jaw fell open. How was Rosalie in this weird Sheet Man dimension with me?

Then it hit me: She was a medium too!

The worst part of the Sheet Man had been his eyes, and what suddenly struck me was that Rosalie now had the same eyes—black pits of tar piercing into my blue ones. It felt like snakes had invaded my

stomach and slithered through my intestines. I knew
Rosalie was bad, but I hadn't expected this.

"He found us out, dear," Rosalie said quietly,
her voice somehow echoing around the room as she
lightly stroked the Sheet Man's material. "And I'd
been so careful for so long."

The Sheet Man said nothing, and I looked around
for Kristina.

"She's here," Rosalie said, a tight smile forming.
"But I wanted to speak with you alone first."

I saw that whenever her eyes moved, so did the
Sheet Man's, like both sets were controlled by her.

"So Angela told you about our deal," Rosalie said,
"and all about Alfred's last bit of trickery?"

She pulled on the ghost leash, but the Sheet Man
didn't move.

"How on earth did you know that?"

"You have your tricks, Baylor. I have mine." She
tugged on the leash again. "You must look at this
from my point of view," she continued, entirely too
calm for my liking. "You see—"

But I didn't get to see, because I couldn't listen
to this bizarre demon-woman for another moment,
especially not when she had supernatural tricks hidden up her sleeve. I cracked open the egg, grabbed
the stone, and chucked it at the Sheet Man.

The sheet unraveled itself like a tornado of cloth, spinning upward to reveal Alfred and a balled-up Kristina, and then ripping itself into shreds to tie around Rosalie in midsentence. They bound her feet, pinned her arms to her sides, and covered her mouth, making her resemble a very haphazardly assembled mummy.

"You did it!" Kristina yelled, unfolding herself and rising up, her hands balled into fists. "Oh, I knew you would!"

Alfred was beaming at me, and the first thing I noticed was that his eyes were actually a light shade of brown. He looked like a friendly old man, though his nose resembled a small mountain squashed in the middle of his face, and I suddenly thought of his son Will's big nose and laughed. They looked exactly alike.

"This is too funny," I said, feeling slaphappy. "It's so great to see you both."

"Wait." Kristina tensed up and looked through a wall. "We're back in the physical world, and the dogs are coming."

And sure enough, the dogs came bounding from the front door—where they'd been barking at Reverend Henry, who was still outside—and leaped at me, their sharp teeth bared.

Alfred laughed, and a fusion bomb of blue

energy flew from his hand and hit the dogs with a
force so great that they were blasted out the window in a disharmonious concert of broken glass
and pathetic yelps.

"So not fair," Kristina said, shaking her head with
admiration at his blasting abilities.

"I've wanted to do that for years," he said, flexing
his still-glowing fingers.

Reverend Henry rushed to the broken window and
looked in to find me there with Rosalie all tied up.

"Baylor, where did you go?!" he yelled. "You just
disappeared!"

"I was transported to that limbo realm," I said.
"Everything's fine now."

"That's great to know *now*," he said while bending over and huffing, "but I panicked and called
your mom. She's on her way here, and she is *not*
happy with us."

"What?" I moaned. "No!"

"Who cares, Baylor!" Kristina said. "We need to
deal with this whole situation first."

She motioned to Rosalie and Alfred. Their eyes
were back to normal, and I was so relieved never to
have to look at those beady black eyes ever again.

"Thank you so much, Baylor," Alfred said, practically dancing around the room in celebration of his

freedom. "My lovely ex-wife had been using some voodoo magic for years before I died, and I was trapped in that gray landscape the second I crossed over."

Rosalie tried to say something, but her mouth was tightly gagged.

"It's not so great being bound up, is it, dear?" he said.

She glared at him, but her now unremarkable eyes affected no one.

Reverend Henry, unaware of the two ghosts present, kept looking from me to the bound-and-gagged Rosalie in shock. "What? Bay—wha—how—are you serious? What is this?"

"Just settling some grisly ghost business, Reverend," I said, grinning dreamily.

"I'll ask you for just one favor, Baylor," Alfred said, turning back to me. "If you wouldn't mind going downstairs to the basement and destroying her hate shrine dedicated to me?"

I looked at Kristina, who was also grinning like a fool, and she nodded.

"Okay," I said, and he led the way down the hall and into the kitchen.

"It's just down there, in the far left corner," he said, pointing to a door next to the refrigerator. "I'd go with you, but you'll forgive me for being a bit paranoid about being so close to evil so soon. I can still feel it lingering all over me."

"I'll come with you," Kristina said, and she flicked something in my mind to tune me into the spirits.

I frowned at her, wondering why she wanted me tuned in, and we walked down the stairs. I found the light switch, and the air was sucked out of my lungs.

Rosalie had erected a table in the corner covered in all kinds of paraphernalia: an ancient, thick book, tarot cards, a cracked mirror, dark prisms, and a small voodoo doll covered in a white sheet, with pins sticking into all parts of the body.

Standing guard over the table was a Bruton, its black, jagged wings spread apart like a massive bat's, taking up nearly the entire width of the basement. The fire in its eyes burned mercilessly.

"Kristina," I said under my breath. "Back up. Go back up."

"No. Walk over with confidence and destroy the relics," she said, defiant.

I started walking slowly again, and with every step the fire in the Bruton's eyes glowed more sinisterly.

"Good demon," I said breathlessly. "Good boy. Please don't attack me."

Its head followed me and shifted violently around, like black smoke escaping into the air.

I focused on my breathing, trying to keep it steady, in and out.

It can't hurt you, I reminded myself. *It can't touch you.*

I collected the tarot cards as the Bruton hovered over me, maybe three feet away. I ripped them up, trying to stifle a horrified gasp as wisps of black energy slithered into the air from the paper shreds and circled my hands, as if trying to invade me, before ultimately returning to the demon. Then I threw the book onto the floor and chucked the mirror at it, a thousand pieces of glass stabbing into its cover and scattering all over the bare gray concrete; the prisms met the same fate a few seconds later

Finally, the doll. With each needle I removed, more black energy returned to the Bruton, like he was vacuuming it up. I shredded the miniature sheet, then ripped the head off the ragged voodoo doll, threw the pieces down, and stomped on them.

The table empty, I smiled at Kristina and said, "That wasn't so bad."

The Bruton, which had been eerily watching me, suddenly screeched, and it was like an airplane had just crashed into the house. The fire in its eyes exploded out at me, and it started beating its wings back and forth to direct the flames all around me.

"Run, Baylor!" Kristina yelled.

"Where?" I shouted back, seeing only fire, which seemed to take alternating shapes of people writhing in pain.

Kristina looked around, then stuck her hand out and tried to blast a spot through the wall of fire, but it was like water evaporating in the heat of the flames.

The wall started closing in, eviscerating the table and chairs, and before I knew it, the intense heat was just a few feet away, the hairs on my arms burning, the skin practically melting off me. The terror etched in Kristina's face was sinking in, and I closed my eyes and simply thought, *Help*.

A white flash lit up the circle of fire, and Colonel Fleetwood dropped down from nowhere, wielding his silver battle sword. He cut through the flames and thrust the sword forward into the body of the Bruton.

The fire instantly vanished, reabsorbed into the shrieking Bruton. With one final fiery gaze, it tilted its head at me—at least, I think it did—and, wings beating furiously, flew off to terrorize someone else.

"Demon dung," Kristina and I said in unison. We looked at each other and laughed nervously.

"Thank you, Colonel Fleetwood," I said.

"The pleasure was all mine, Baylor, now that I can freely travel between sides again," he said. He looked Kristina up and down. She was the closest to crying I'd ever seen.

"I don't know what happened," she said.

"The protections are currently dismal at best," the colonel said. "We'll need to reinforce them later today."

"Baylor was almost taken by a Bruton," Kristina shrieked. "We should do it right now."

Before the colonel could say anything else, though, Reverend Henry's bloodcurdling scream bellowed from upstairs.

22

Seriously, avoid Brutons at all costs.

"WHAT HAPPENED?" I YELLED, SPRINTING up the stairs to the kitchen. "Can either of you see?"

Colonel Fleetwood disappeared, but Kristina stuck with me. I sprinted down the hall to the living room, where Rosalie was standing behind Reverend Henry, holding a sharp dagger to his neck. Alfred and the colonel hovered near them.

"Blast her!" I yelled.

"The knife is right against his throat," Kristina said. "The force would cut his head off."

"How did she get out?"

"The dark energy of that demon slashed her bindings off," Alfred said.

"The Bruton!" Anger detonated inside of me. "I'm going to hunt it down and banish it."

"Baylor, let's focus on the situation at hand," Kristina said warily.

"Right," I said, looking at the reverend's distraught and very confused face. "Rosalie, you insane witch of a person, drop the knife right now."

"Baylor Bosco, I knew the second you showed up on my doorstep that you'd be a thorn in my side," she said. "Although I should have realized that the first time my dear Alfred escaped to visit you."

"You escaped her to see me?" I said to Alfred.

"I did, though it didn't accomplish anything except to terrify you," he said. "Sorry about that. I needed to pass on a message to you somehow but couldn't find a way."

"Why did you almost kill me on Halloween, then?"

"That was me," Rosalie said brightly. "Once I realized what he'd done, I decided to send my own message."

"And then you showed me the shoes," I said to Alfred, "knowing Angela was back in town and had dropped them off."

"He certainly did," Rosalie hissed.

"I can't believe you can communicate with ghosts," I said, shaking my head. If my purpose in life was to help people, surely hers couldn't have been much different. "How could you treat someone this way?"

"Unlike you, dear," she spit, "this curse is not something I'm proud of."

"Clearly, since you're holding a reverend hostage with a knife at the moment."

"He's my insurance," she said. "With him as my hostage, you'll do whatever I demand."

"You can't go five minutes without terrorizing someone, you psychopath," Alfred said, sounding amused.

"Now that you're dead, *dear*, your opinion is worth even less to me than it was when you were alive," she said.

"Fantastic," he said. "Then it certainly won't interest you to know that Baylor's mother is almost here with a police cruiser close behind."

Her eyes flashed in shock, and she bit her lip. "Well, it looks like this will have to be fast, then. Baylor, now that you've taken away my puppet, you're going to help me get the money Angela owes me."

"That's not going to happen," I said.

"It is," she said, "because if you don't, I'll find you, and I will hurt your family." She smiled. "And I know you wouldn't want that."

"Are you insane?" I asked.

"The answer is clearly yes," Kristina said.

"Be quiet, you dumb girl," Rosalie spit. "I thought once I had you out of the way, Baylor would be too stupid to figure any of this out. I was wrong about that, but since I know he was so dedicated to finding his dead sister, it's not too big of a leap to guess he'll be just as dedicated to keeping his family alive."

She grinned horribly, revealing her straight, coffee-stained teeth, while Reverend Henry's hands gestured by his sides. He had remained silent the whole time, since he couldn't totally follow the conversation taking place with the ghosts, but he now started to give me a strange look with exaggerated wide eyes, his lips clenched together in a white line.

"What?" I asked slowly, trying to pick up his clues. "If I don't help, you're going to kill Reverend Henry? Or are you going to keep him alive and hurt my family? Which is it?"

That's when the reverend smiled. That was it! Of all people, he was the one most familiar with the ramblings of lunatics, and he could recognize a crazy woman without a plan from a mile away. Without wasting another second, I took off through the door and ran as fast as I could down the street.

"Stop!" she screamed.

I sprinted around the corner and down Main Street. Kristina was gliding next to me a second later.

"She's getting in her car," she said. "She's going to chase you down."

"The police will be here any minute," I said, panting. "She should leave town before she gets arrested for attempted murder of a holy man!"

"She's not thinking clearly," she said. "She wants that money, and she doesn't want her kids to know what she's done."

I veered into the tackle shop I'd visited with my dad on Sunday. "Call the police!" I yelled to the cashier. "A crazy lady with a knife is chasing me."

"I knew I should have stayed in bed this morning!" said the cashier, lifting up the phone and dialing 911.

"Keep running, Baylor," Kristina said suddenly.

"Do you have another exit?" I asked. The cashier nodded furiously, pointing to a door in the back of the store. "Lock your doors!" I yelled, and took off running.

I passed through a small office and clambered out the door, where there was a squat-looking ghost with hair twisted into a tight bun standing in the back alley. She looked sort of familiar, and my face must have tipped her off that I recognized her, because she sneered at me.

"You should have helped me when I asked," she said. Then it clicked—she was the ghost Kristina vanquished when I woke up in the hospital. Before I could say anything, she yelled out, "They're back here!" her voice amplified like she was talking into a megaphone.

"Argh!" Kristina yelled, stretching out both hands and blasting the ghost with blue energy; the woman flitted her fingers sarcastically as she faded away. "*Now* it decides to work," she mumbled, clearly still bitter about the Bruton. "Run faster, Baylor."

I took off again and tried my best to sprint, but I didn't know the area well and wasn't sure which way would be the best route.

"Left or right?" I said, as the road I was on was about to dead-end.

"Right! Stay hidden, but stay close to the crowded areas!"

I circled back to Main Street, wondering where Rosalie was. I was sprinting down the street, in the opposite direction from her house, when her car came screeching from a side street and stopped a foot short of hitting me.

"Stop, Baylor," she hissed, exiting the car. "Listen to me. You will help me, or you will never be free of me. Ever."

"He'll be fine," Kristina said. "You don't stand a chance against me and my spirit guides."

"Tell that to the Bruton who nearly burned your brother to a crisp," she said.

Kristina's mouth dropped open a little, but she kept her cool. "I'd be happy to."

Alfred appeared next to us.

"Leave the child alone, you monster," he said, getting in Rosalie's face. "Haven't you done enough damage?"

"Get out of here, Alfred," she said, her eyes hungry for me. "This no longer concerns you. You can cross over to the Beyond now."

"Rosalie, you idiot, I knew the whole time Angela was working with you, and I liked it," he said. "I liked having a young, beautiful girl fawning over me in my last years."

Rosalie's face was motionless. "What?"

"You think I didn't have anyone watching you after you didn't get any of my money in the divorce? I knew what you were up to the whole time. I asked Angela not to split the money with you as my dying wish."

"You knew? And you left me and your children with nothing?"

"Of course not. The children have trusts," he said. "They'll be granted access on their thirtieth birthdays."

Rosalie swallowed hard. "You left the kids money?"

"Yes, and do you know what?" He took a step forward, like he was threatening her. "They probably would have been more than happy to share it with you. But not after they find out everything you've done."

Her eyes targeted me, and the crazy rage had grown manic. "You can't tell them."

"Oh? Is that how this is going to work now?" I said. "And you're going to stop me how, exactly? Both the reverend and I know about what you did. Are you going to kill us both?"

She was silent for a moment, her eyes never leaving mine. Then, originating from somewhere deep within her, somewhere infernal, a shrill, inhuman scream erupted from her mouth, and black energy shot out of her hands and straight at my chest. Alfred leaped in front of it, and he screamed in agony and dropped to the asphalt as the Bruton descended to Rosalie's side.

That was my cue to run.

"It's time for this to end, Baylor," she growled from somewhere too close behind.

Kristina tried to blast her back, but the Bruton effortlessly absorbed the energy, fanning the flames in its eyes.

"Fleetwood, we need your help!" Kristina yelled.

I looked back to see Rosalie chasing me with the knife, her arm stretched out and slashing wildly just a few feet behind. I wondered if anyone could see this, if anyone else thought this looked as absolutely insane as I did. Where were the police? Where were the people to help? Had Rosalie's evil power distracted them? Had she utilized the Bruton to do her bidding without us realizing it?

I sprinted past the last of the shops and turned down a busy road, Rosalie hot on my heels.

"You can't win, Baylor!" she said.

I didn't say anything but heard a grunt a moment later. I looked back to find the knife hurtling at my head, but Fleetwood appeared and swatted it down with a flash of his sword.

"You British maggot!" she said, picking the knife up off the road.

Kristina gasped, looking into the distance ahead.

"What is it?" I said.

"Run as fast as you can, Baylor!"

"What is it, Kristina?"

But she was gone. Where did she go? What did she mean? What on earth was I running from now?

Rosalie continued chasing me down the empty street, flanked by Alfred, Fleetwood, and the Bruton, a flurry of black, blue, and white energy passing back and forth between them, and we traversed another twenty yards before the first car I'd seen the whole time finally appeared from behind a hill up ahead.

It was my mom's SUV. I had no idea what Kristina had planned, but I remembered her words and commanded my legs to pump harder and faster than they'd ever worked before, rocketing me forward, away from Rosalie.

Fifty feet.

Thirty feet.

Ten feet.

A half second later I closed my eyes and leaped forward as my mom's car swerved left, cutting just behind me. I could feel the wind from her car pushing me forward, and then a piercing scream hit my ears, followed by a terrible thud.

My mom scrambled out of the car, not sure whether to run to me or to check out the scene on the other side of her car.

"Oh my God! Oh my God!" she screamed over and over as she decided to run to me first. "I don't know what happened."

"Connie Bosco, you need to calm down and get back in the car," I said. Rosalie could be creeping around the corner to attack us at any moment. I

grabbed her arm and threw her into the backseat. I
lunged in behind her, locked the doors, and crawled
past her to the other side to survey the scene.

Rosalie was slowly getting up and looking around.
It was a brutal sight. Her face was covered in blood,
and her expression was more savage than ever.

"We need to call for help! She's probably hurt," my
mom said.

"Mom, she was chasing me with a knife," I said.
"She's not the one who needs help."

"It's still not safe for you," Kristina said, appearing
in the car. "Tell Mom to hit the gas!"

"You don't need to tell me twice," I said. "Mom,
get in the driver's seat and get us outta here."

She started to protest and motioned to Rosalie,
who was now reaching for the knife. "But what about
that—"

"Kristina just said we're in danger and need to go!"

I'd said the magic words. She crawled into the
front seat and shifted gears. We'd made it about three
feet when Kristina and I both gasped simultaneously.

My mom slammed on the brakes. "What's going on?"

She couldn't see it, but the Bruton had glided over
and latched on to Rosalie with its fingers, if you
could call those black, talonlike appendages fingers.

"What are you doing?" Rosalie screamed as black

smoke rose from the point where the fingers were touching her. "Stop it!"

"What's happening to her? What's that smoke coming from her arm?" my mom whispered in fright.

"The time has come for you to repay your debts," the Bruton said with a crackly, deep voice, like a blazing fire pit come to life.

"But I'm not finished here!" Rosalie screamed, her voice earsplitting.

"We say otherwise." Its wings beating vigorously, the demon ascended toward the sky with Rosalie in its clutches, like a squiggling mouse caught in the talons of an owl, away from both the physical world and the Beyond, to a place Kristina and I knew little about. The last thing we heard from her was one long, anguished scream.

"How is that woman flying?" Mom yelped. She looked at me in horror. "You can't fly, right, Baylor? Please tell me you can't fly."

I shook my head. "Definitely not."

The police arrived shortly after, and I felt justified in my thinking that the Bruton had kept them from getting there faster when they mentioned how their sirens had caused three different car accidents, delaying their journey into town.

"Hey, you're that ghost kid!" one of the officers said, a goofy smile on his face.

"Uh, yeah, I am," I said.

"See any ghosts around now?" he asked excitedly, looking from left to right as though he might be able to spot one passing by.

His grandmother swatted him on the hand. "Tell Patty-cakes to shut up and do his job."

"Your grandmother would like me to say, 'Patty-cakes, shut up and do your job.'"

The color drained from his face. He pulled out a notepad and coughed a little. "All right, sir, let's get your statement."

23

And most importantly: Be brave.

THE NEXT FEW DAYS WERE INTERESTING, to say the least.

Mom was featured in the local news as a hero who saved her baby boy from a crazy woman who had somehow evaded capture and was on the loose, and the story made national news when they realized the baby boy was none other than yours truly, Baylor Bosco, the weirdo extraordinaire who could speak to ghosts.

Once that happened, reporters camped outside my house, looking for me to give them any sort of material. They wanted the wondrous boy medium to deliver healing messages on camera, which I politely declined. They asked if I was nervous that Rosalie Parker—or as she'd been known since the divorce, Rosalie Timmons—might come out of hiding and attack me, but when I told them that a demon had taken her away, they laughed like I was joking.

There were long days filled with police questioning for me, my mom, and Reverend Henry, but in the end there was nothing to be done. Rosalie was gone. My mom felt indirectly responsible for Rosalie's disappearance, since she'd swerved in front of Rosalie and precipitated her capture by the Bruton, but I reminded her that Rosalie had been chasing me down the street and trying to kill me. I asked Kristina why the Bruton had taken Rosalie away so suddenly, but she shrugged and said, "The evil play by a different set of rules."

The best part was getting to talk to Will and Isabella Parker. They came to Keene devastated and distraught, but with Alfred's assistance I got to tell them the truth they'd been waiting years to hear.

In a matter of minutes they went from destroyed over their mother's disappearance, to horrified by the news of what she'd been doing, to overwhelmed with joy over the revelation that their father had known exactly what he was doing.

"Tell Isabella she can finally move back home,"

Alfred said, gazing affectionately at his sobbing daughter. He was still battered from Rosalie's black-energy attack, but Kristina said he'd be fine eventually. "She has nothing to run from anymore."

He also gave me permission to spoil the news of their trusts. They were going to get a special letter on their thirtieth birthdays, but he decided that now would be as good a time as ever to reveal the news. That led to more crying and joyous outbursts, followed by one more message from Alfred.

"Find Angela," I said to them. "She made your dad very happy, and he'd like for you to have a relationship."

Their faces tightened, but they didn't protest.

Keene High School's homecoming game was that weekend, and since my dad was a teacher there, he liked for the whole family to attend. My parents, unfortunately, hadn't forgotten about my disaster with Aunt Hilda, so this year they invited her to come along with my grandparents as a gesture of goodwill. It was a cold night, the first time we had to break out the winter gear and bundle up, and I hoped Aunt Hilda would be wearing too many layers to be able to speak.

The night was going smoothly until some freshman

girls spotted me in the stands after the band's half-
time show and started clamoring for messages. Since
I'd been on the news so much, the number of Bay-
lievers had skyrocketed. Meanwhile, Aunt Hilda sat
there with a big frown plastered on her wrinkly face,
suddenly fascinated with the gum stuck to the metal
bleachers by her feet.

I had delivered a few messages when a woman
with the same attitude as Aunt Hilda spoke up. She
had blond hair that was cut short above her shoulders, and she turned around to look at me down
her nose.

"Honey, I have a close relationship with my
maker," she said with a condescending grin, "and I
know where you'll be going if you keep up this spirit
nonsense." She pointed down to the ground.

"Hey, now," my dad said, "there's no need to be
rude, Mrs. Jalasky."

"I'm just stating my beliefs, sir," she said, turning
back around.

My dad was about to say something else, but I
put my hand on his shoulder and tried not to laugh
out loud. The woman's father was standing next to
her, rolling his eyes and saying, "Do you hear this
girl? Can you believe I raised someone so closed-
minded?"

"Give him something specific to say to her," Kristina said, nudging him.

"Tell Tammie she shouldn't be judging you when *she's* the one who's been buying five bottles of wine every weekend instead of donating that money to people who actually need it."

"I can't say that," I murmured, blushing.

"And one more thing, Mr. Bosco," Tammie said, turning around yet again. "Now that I know the beliefs you instill in your children, I can't say I'm too thrilled about my son having you for his teacher."

My dad's eyes flickered in shock, and I knew he was thinking of his dad. He'd finally confessed to me that Grandpa's message was about his insecurity over changing jobs. I guess he'd been worried about the fact that he wasn't making as much money working as a teacher, but it made him happier than working as an accountant.

Seeing the pain in my dad's eyes, I was suddenly furious with the woman. "Hey, Tammie," I said, enunciating every syllable, "your dad says to lay off the weekend wine and donate the money to people who need it instead."

The woman's jaw dropped dramatically, and Kristina, giggling, let me see her red, embarrassed aura.

"How dare you!" she said, looking around at the

other moms, who were staring at her awkwardly, her blond hair smacking her face. "I should sue you for slander."

"Ask her to let you sniff her 'water bottle,'" her dad said, making air quotations with his fingers.

"Tammie, your dad thinks you should let me smell your water bottle," I said quietly. "Any reason why?"

The muscles in her neck flared, and she got up, grabbed her purse, and stomped away as the football players ran back onto the field to start the third quarter.

"Well," my dad said, a little smile on his face, "that was embarrassing."

After the game ended, I was holding Ella and walking next to Aunt Hilda, who was hobbling along with her walker. The only sound was Ella's gurgling.

"Did you have fun, Aunt Hilda?" I finally asked.

"Sure," she scoffed. "I especially enjoyed the half-time entertainment."

My cheeks flushed, and I was fed up. "Is there a reason you don't like me, Aunt Hilda?"

Her eyebrows shot up, and almost as soon as I finished speaking, she blurted out, "Why haven't you ever delivered a message from Marvy?" She nervously caressed her half-heart necklace, and for the first time I noticed the letters *MAR* lightly etched onto the pendant.

"Her husband, Uncle Marvin," Kristina said, wafting back from eavesdropping on a conversation Jack was having with my dad. Her voice was ominous. "I've never seen him before. I don't think he's in the Beyond, Baylor. . . ."

"Uh, I'm sorry, Aunt Hilda, but he's never appeared to me," I said. "I can't make him deliver a message if he doesn't want to." I paused. "Or maybe he can't deliver one."

She stopped walking and reached into her pocket for her handkerchief. "I wish he would."

She blew her nose while Kristina and I exchanged awkward glances. If Uncle Marvin wasn't in the Beyond, then he was somewhere else . . . somewhere bad. Maybe even with Rosalie.

"Sorry," I said quietly.

Then we kept walking like nothing had happened.

The Fall Ball was less than a week away, and Aiden and J had successfully avoided talking to each other for several days. But no longer could they avoid the subject.

As far as I knew, J had said no to Andrew but still hadn't said yes to Aiden. Aiden had gotten out of his mess by telling Cassie he could never be with someone who would attack one of his friends.

But even though they had no attachments precluding them from getting together, they still weren't together.

"This is getting pathetic," Kristina said as she sat with us at lunch and watched Aiden eat his pepperoni sandwich in sad silence. "It's even worse than listening to Napoléon perform his speeches over and over again." She shook her head. "And nothing has ever been worse than that."

"Well, what are we going to do?" I muttered. She did a double take. She wasn't used to me responding to her questions at school.

"We've got to make him man up, like you said J wanted."

We watched him use a pepperoni to wipe mustard off his lip and then eat it.

I tried to hide my disgust. Kristina didn't have to worry about that and looked at him as though he'd just sneezed in her face.

"You're going to have to help him again," she said. "I'm sorry, but it's just the way it is. Remember last year's jazz concert, when you all performed with that soloist?"

"Yeah?"

"Well, you should perform it, and Aiden can be the soloist," she said with a devilish grin.

And the image bloomed so clearly in my mind that I thought it just might work. I ran to the band room, grabbed my tuba, and brought it back to the table.

"What are you doing with that?" Aiden asked.

"Aiden, I'm helping you redeem yourself with J," I said.

"What's going on? What are you talking about?" he asked, panicked.

"Remember that jazz concert from last year? That funny love song we did?"

"Yeah," he said slowly, "we had that pretty singer from the high school perform with us."

"Well, you get to be a pretty singer for a few minutes."

"What?" he squeaked, and I thought I saw tears spring to his eyes. "Baylor, no, you can't do this to me!"

But the bell rang, and I already had my tuba, and Kristina was goading me on, and J was walking in our direction.

"Sorry, buddy!" I said sincerely. "In three, two, one."

And I began playing the notes, while a couple of our band friends pushed him to stand on the table.

"Oh my God," he said, his legs suffering from an earthquake only he could feel.

J was looking at Aiden with alarmed intrigue, which I took as a good sign.

"Now!" I said to Aiden between breaths.

"I'm wise to you baby," Aiden croaked, completely out of tune and speaking instead of singing, his arms stiff at his sides. "Think that I'm going away."

J walked slowly our way, and I played my tuba with gusto. Bobby ran over, laughing, and starting drumming the beat on a textbook.

"People call me craaazy, at least for today."

She smiled, and miraculously Aiden smiled and started singing with an air of confidence, looking only at J while everyone around us snickered.

"When you say you don't waaaant me, it makes me feel bluuuue."

Kristina jumped up as J stopped a few feet from us. "It's working!"

"If you don't believe I looooove you, look what a fool I've beeeen! If you don't think I'm siiiiinking, look whaaat a hole I'm in!"

Aiden climbed down from the table and grabbed her hands.

"Before I met you, I had a good pair of shooooes, but take a look at me now!" He let go of J, stepped back, and kicked off his shoes, falling to his knees dramatically. "I've got the barefooted bluuuues!"

Everyone around us was cheering and whooping, and Aiden reached up for J's hands again and pulled her down to the ground with him. Kristina touched my shoulder and told me to stop playing, and I motioned for Bobby to stop too.

Looking her right in the eyes, a small smile on his face, Aiden sang the last line: "If you don't believe I love you . . ."—he swallowed, trying to keep his voice from cracking—"look what a fool I've been."

There was a moment of silence where J and Aiden stared at each other, and everyone else stared at them in jealousy, and everyone was wondering what was going to happen next. Then J smiled, leaned in, and kissed Aiden on the cheek, and the crowd exploded.

A bunch of girls came up and started gushing to me.

"That was the most romantic thing I've ever seen."

"You're so talented, Baylor!"

"You're just so blessed!"

"Do you have a date for the dance this weekend?"

I looked at Kristina, who was grimacing next to me, grossed out I was getting attention from girls. She nodded at me to talk to them, so I smiled, embarrassed, and tried to answer them politely. Bobby sauntered over and said, "This fine gentleman is up for grabs, and Baylor is too. Any takers?" The girls giggled, and I blushed almost as bad as Aiden.

The truth was, I didn't have a date. I'd been so
distracted by the Sheet Man escapades that I was
planning on going alone, or possibly with Aiden if
he and J hadn't made up by then. But really, I wasn't
going alone. I'd be going with Kristina.

Except . . . she was my sister, and dead or alive,
that was still weird.

"Don't feel bad for me," she said, as though she
could read my mind. "I can ask Colonel Fleetwood
to accompany me that night."

I smiled at her and turned back to the girls.

If I could get a date out of it, why not?

The night of the dance, before my mom took me
to J's house, where a bunch of us were meeting to
take pictures, I gathered my family in our backyard,
much to their chagrin. It hadn't snowed yet, but the
temperature was so low that we were one spilled cup
of water away from having snow.

We huddled together by one of the bushes, and
for once Kristina had no idea what I was about to do.
I had secretly recruited Madame Nadirah to help me.

"What's this about, Baylor?" my mom asked as she
clung on to my dad for warmth.

"So, family, as you all know, I can see and speak
to Kristina," I said, holding something heavy and

wrapped in a towel, "and even though you can't see or hear her, she's constantly around and very much a part of our lives."

"Baylor, what are you doing?" Kristina asked, sounding embarrassed.

"And I thought it was sad that there wasn't a tangible reminder of her in our house, so I decided to change that."

I put the object down on some mulch and took the towel off to reveal a flat rock with an inscription: FOR KRISTINA, OUR BELOVED DAUGHTER AND SISTER, WHOSE LOVE LIVES ON IN OUR HEARTS.

"There," I said. "Now no one can ever forget you."

Kristina, looking grateful that ghosts can't cry, walked over and melted into me, sending chills all throughout my body.

"I hate when you do that!" I said, backing away.

Ella laughed. "Kristi hug!" she screamed in my brother's arms, and I ran my fingers through her curly hair.

"That's right!" I said. "Kristina gave me a hug."

I looked over at my mom, who was breathing deeply and nodding.

"That was so nice, Baylor," she said softly as we walked back inside. "After all she's done for us, I can't believe we didn't have anything like it before."

"I sort of can," my dad said, wrapping his arm around her waist, "if only because we were too sad to create one."

"Well, this surprise was mainly for her," I said, my voice barely containing my excitement. "I've got one more for you two."

My parents glanced at each other, worried, as I opened the hall closet and handed them a wrapped box. "Open it!"

My mom tore off the wrapping paper slowly, my dad at her side. The paper floated to the ground as they stared in shock at the framed portrait of Kristina.

I had made some friends at the police station, which is to say I charmed them by delivering endless messages from their loved ones, and one of them knew a sketch artist, who agreed to help me draw Kristina. However, it turned out that I wasn't very good at describing Kristina's features, so the frustrated artist left me alone in a back room to search through a database to find the facial features that looked most like Kristina's. It was boring at first, but as I scrolled through pages and pages of noses, I got to ask Kristina over and over about a lot of the things that'd been bugging me about her world.

"But what can you *do*? Tommy specifically said you weren't an average ghost," I said, flipping through nose after nose on the computer, trying to find one that matched hers. "It's not fair. You know I can talk to ghosts, so I should get to know whatever makes you special in the Beyond."

"Tommy needs to learn to keep his mouth shut," Kristina snapped. She still hadn't gotten over him advising me to venture into that weird limbo by myself. "All I can say is that I get to learn lessons in the Beyond."

"But everyone learns lessons in the Beyond. You say that all the time."

She shrugged.

"Do you go into a classroom and listen to someone talk and take notes? Who's the teacher? Is it Gandhi? It's totally Gandhi, isn't it?"

"Baylor, stop."

"And Grandpa Bosco said that being ghostnapped by the Sheet Man was part of your journey. What does that mean? How was being trapped in a bunch of sheets for a week beneficial to you at all?"

"Baylor," she finally said after the fiftieth time I'd asked, "listen to me."

I looked up from all the noses and smiled politely as she walked over and crouched down next to me. "Yes, ma'am."

"I truly don't know that much more than you, but I

promise we'll both find out more as we walk through this life together," she said, smiling widely, like she was looking forward to it or something. "We're a duo, Baylor. The undead duo! And this really is just the beginning. We have so, *so* much more to learn."

In the end the sketch artist and I had finally come up with a pretty accurate depiction of Kristina. The long hair, the skinny face that matched my mother's, the kind eyes that so resembled Ella's, Jack's funny nose, the flat mouth of my father, and my round chin.

"This . . . this can't be . . . ," my mom said, shaking her head, tears streaming freely down her face. It's a good thing we weren't outside, or else they'd have turned into icicles. "Kristina?"

I nodded. The cold weather must have really dried my eyes out, because they were suddenly flooded with water too.

My dad studied the portrait in silence, his eyes moving rapidly, his head nodding to a fast beat only he could hear.

Kristina stood off to the side, staring happily. She had been embarrassed at first about the idea, but the more she thought about it, the more she wanted them to have it. In fact, it was supposed to be their Christmas present, but she was so pleased with how it turned out and so eager for them to finally see her, she said she'd help me find something even better. Watching my parents' reactions, I realized I'd been duped.

"She's beautiful," my mom whispered.

We stared at the picture for a few more minutes, until my mom shook her head fast and said, "It's time to go, Baylor! You're going to be late for pictures!" She sounded giddy and ran to clean up her mascara so she could look nice for all the other parents. "We still have to pick up the corsage, too!"

At the florist's shop my mom and I watched as the woman behind the counter bounced with excitement.

"I just love all these dances the school puts on!" she said as she wrapped up the corsage. "It's so cute to see the kids get all dressed up and pick up flowers and act all nervous."

"I'm not nervous!" I said, and my voice picked that exact moment to crack. She winked me, and I blushed.

Just as we were leaving, a nice grandma ghost tapped my shoulder.

"I'm sorry, young man, I know you're busy," she said, smiling in a sheepish way. "But I was hoping you might tell my daughter how proud I am of her for chasing her dreams and owning her own flower shop." She looked down at some lush yellow roses and smiled sadly. "I so wish I could smell these. They've always been my favorite."

I looked at my watch, and Kristina smiled and said, "It'll only take a minute."

"Hold on, Mom," I said. "Duty calls."

I turned back to the counter and smiled at the florist. "One more thing, ma'am," I said. "My name is Baylor Bosco, and I can communicate with people who have crossed over."

Acknowledgments

TO MY WONDERFUL PARENTS—I ALREADY dedicated this book to you. What more do you want?! I'm kidding. Thanks for your endless love and support. I'm not sure how I got so lucky to deserve such a great mom and dad, but I'm not going to question it. Ben and Jenny, my dear siblings, thank you for the many years of fighting and yelling and emotional scarring from when we were growing up. You've provided *plenty* of material for future books. (Just kidding again! I'm on a roll. Love ya.)

All my thanks and gratitude to my agent, Dan Lazar—the best in the biz—for being generally awesome, relentlessly tenacious, and totally game to answer my e-mails at all times of day. Thanks to everyone else at Writers House, especially Torie Doherty-Munro, Cecilia de la Campa, and Angharad Kowal.

To my editor, Michael Strother—thanks so much for all your hard work. Where would I be without your fantastic, insightful notes? Well, we're about to find out, since your talents have taken you elsewhere! However, I'm thrilled Amy Cloud has taken over editorial duties and I look forward to working with someone so delightfully warmhearted and smart. Thanks to everyone else at S&S/Aladdin, especially Mara Anastas, Audrey Gibbons, Jodie Hockensmith, Mary Marotta, and Carolyn Swerdloff. Oh, and of course, thanks to Hugh D'Andrade, for creating a cover that perfectly captures the spirit of the book.

Thanks to my family, friends, teachers, coworkers, and countless other people for all your support and kind words of encouragement. Huge thanks to Sue Davis, Seema Mahanian, and Lauren Vallario for your invaluable input and guidance.

I'd be remiss not to acknowledge anything and everything that's helped me along from, well, the other side. My long-lost twin, wherever you are, thanks for the inspiration. Theresa Caputo, my other vital source of inspiration—you are a gem. And, finally, a special shout-out to Grandpa Erv, Uncle Moose, and Mr. Senior—thanks for keeping watch over me.